CRUSH

ALSO BY GARY PAULSEN

GARY PAULSEN

CRUSH

The Theory, Practice and Destructive Properties of Love

WENDY
LAMB
BOOKS

Text copyright © 2012 by Gary Paulsen
Jacket art copyright © 2012 by James Bernardin

All rights reserved. Published in the United States by Wendy Lamb Books, an imprint of Random House Children's Books, a division of Random House, Inc., New York.

Wendy Lamb Books and the colophon are trademarks of Random House, Inc.

Visit us on the Web! randomhouse.com/kids

Educators and librarians, for a variety of teaching tools, visit us at randomhouse.com/teachers

Library of Congress Cataloging-in-Publication Data is available upon request.
ISBN 978-0-385-74230-6 (trade)
ISBN 978-0-375-99054-0 (lib. bdg.)
ISBN 978-0-307-97453-2 (ebook)

Printed in the United States of America

10 9 8 7 6 5 4 3 2 1

First Edition

*This book is dedicated to my
friends at Gilda's Club and
St. Philip's Academy in
Newark, New Jersey,
and to Betsy Buell,
who brought us all together.*

Foreword

I'm the most romantic guy you'll ever meet.

Potentially, that is.

I'm only fourteen, but I've known for as long as I can remember that love makes the world go round, love is all there is, love is all you need. They're universal rules. Cosmic inevitabilities.

If you ask me, people who aren't in touch with what it takes to be a great date are just heathens.

I guess I should admit that I don't actually have a girlfriend at the moment. In fact, I've never even gone out on a date. Still, I don't think that's the gold standard for determining if a guy would make a good boyfriend or not.

See, I've learned that the best way to make other people like you is to show them how great you think they are. I've been practicing this technique on my family and friends; it's not romantic, of course, but it's good experience for when I eventually have a girlfriend. I'm working up to romance. Someday. I think that's where a lot of guys go wrong; they don't develop sufficient interpersonal skills before they start dating.

I know I have the potential to excel at romance because I'm thoughtful, charming and considerate with people who are important to me.

To my best friend, JonPaul, I've said: "Buddy, you're going to be the only middle school student scouted by Major League Baseball. If there's a record you haven't broken, JonPaul, I don't want to know about it."

To my sorta friend Connie, I've said: "You're going to blow them away when you go to the mock Congress. That electoral-vote bar graph and general-population pie chart you put together were really informative."

To my enemy Katie, I've said: "We're lucky to have an academic role model like you in our class. Those girls were just jealous when they called you a curve-wrecker. Sure, you might skew the average and make the rest of us look bad, but that's our fault for not studying as hard as you do."

Out of context, this all sounds like I might have been laying it on a little thick, but in the heat of the moment, I was gold; JonPaul, Connie and Katie didn't even know it was happening, but my stock was rising in their eyes during those conversations.

I wasn't lying; I don't lie.

Not anymore.

And I wasn't trying to get anyone to do anything for me at their expense. I don't manipulate people.

Not anymore.

But there's nothing wrong with making folks like you by telling them what you know will make them feel better about themselves.

Although I lack what you could call practical experience, I appreciate girls. Or, more precisely, one girl. Tina. Katrina Maria Zabinski, whom I have known most of my life but only noticed recently.

The ideal girlfriend.

Tina's the most beautiful girl I've ever seen; everything about her—hair, face, clothes—looks like an entire glam squad just got done working on her. Her laugh sounds like bells or angels or something so wonderful words haven't been invented yet to describe it. She's got a lot of friends and she actually seems to like them, and they like her, unlike some of the kids in this school, who pick friends based on popularity even if they don't particularly get along.

I'm also the perfect potential boyfriend, a combination of all that I believe girls look for in future dates. I'm understanding and sensitive, but not to the point of looking like I'm close to writing poetry and talking about my feelings. While I'm not a prize athlete like my best buddy, JonPaul, I don't let down my team on the field or the court. I get good grades, but I'm not one of those brainiacs who make you worry they're going to correct your grammar. I do the best with what I've got. Most important, I've got a great outlook on life, and that's got to be a sure way to anyone's heart.

I'm not bragging or conceited, I'm just pointing out the obvious.

Tina and I are perfect for each other.

Of course, it's all in theory right now. I haven't had a chance to break out my inner chivalry yet.

Because the one thing I lack is the experience to know how to let Tina know that I think about her all the time and I'd like to stand close enough to her to smell her hair and I'd like to open doors for her and stand between her and traffic on sidewalks and share private jokes that only she and I get—how to let her know all that without freaking her out that I'm an obsessive, creepy stalker. I'm the kind of guy who'd know exactly the right things to say about her to make her feel so good about herself that she'd start to feel good about me.

I have a knack for reading people and being aware of their feelings, though, so I'm pretty sure all I need to do is put my mind to it and, before I know it, I'll have this romance thing down.

I used to think like that.

Before my life went all kittywampus on me.

1

The Scientific Mind Knows That Science Is the Search for Truth in the Natural World

Although I'd realized six or eight weeks ago that I was crazy about Tina Zabinski and I wanted to go on a date with her the same way I want to keep converting oxygen into carbon dioxide, I'd been playing it cool, taking it slow. I was waiting for the exact right moment to present itself before making my move.

That's better than saying that I couldn't remember how to speak when she came near and I tended to fall down when she noticed me.

I'd planned to ask her out recently; I had the perfect first date in mind, one that would show her how lucky she was to be with a guy like me. The school dance. But I didn't actually ask her. Thought about it, sure; planned to do it, absolutely; came right out and asked, not a chance.

I'd thought I had all the time in the world to work on connecting the mind-mouth function when I was near her. Until I walked into the school cafeteria on Monday and saw some male-model wannabe sitting next to Tina at a lunch table. He was leaning in as he talked to her—close enough to smell her hair—and she laughed at something he said. I knew in an instant that I was in deep trouble. And that I'd run out of time.

I went straight to my best buddy, JonPaul, who was sprinkling extra wheat germ on his organic peanut butter and raw honey sandwich. JonPaul is a health nut.

"Who's that?" I tilted my head toward Tina's table.

"The new kid."

"What new kid?"

"Cash Devine."

"That's his actual name?"

"Yup."

"You're kidding."

"Nope."

"That's the fakest thing I ever heard."

JonPaul shrugged and swallowed a handful of vitamins with his soy milk.

"How do you know him?" I asked.

"He's in my math class."

"What's he doing at Tina's table?"

"She was assigned to show him around school, help get him familiar with everything."

"Since when did a welcome guide become standard operating procedure around here?"

"I dunno. Are those organic grapes in your lunch? And if they are, can I have them? I haven't been getting enough fiber lately and the skins would really help me out."

"Yeah." I shoved what I knew to be run-of-the-mill produce reeking of pesticides toward him as fast as I could, trying to avoid a conversation about what happens to JonPaul's digestive tract when he's fiber-deprived. Been there, done that, have the horrible mental images.

He lined up the grapes next to his baby carrots, Greek yogurt, hardboiled eggs and stone-ground gluten-free crackers. I ate a handful of chocolate-covered potato chips while I studied Tina and the Threat.

Cash caught me looking at him when Tina turned to talk to the girl on her other side, and he headed toward me, a big cheesy grin on his face.

"Cash. Cash Devine. Good to know you."

He sounded like the politicians at the Labor Day parade who hand out mini-flags and ask for your support on Election Day.

"Hey," I grunted back. "Name's Kevin."

"JonPaul," he said, slapping my best friend on the back, "math is gonna be rough, buddy; hope I can count on you for some help."

"Sure."

"Do you know if my guide, Tina, has a boyfriend? She's really hot."

I didn't hear JonPaul's reply; I saw his lips moving, but the pressure in my ears from my brain freak-out deafened me.

No.

No way.

No flipping way.

That plastic-looking, fake-named, phony-friendly doofus wasn't going to waltz into my school and take my girlfriend away from me. Especially when I hadn't had the chance to make her my girlfriend yet.

10

I had to get away from Cash before I did something embarrassing, like slug him or watch my head explode all over JonPaul's surgeon general–approved lunch. I mumbled some excuse about getting a homework assignment and bailed.

I saw my friends Katie and Connie and made a beeline for their table. Okay, I'm stretching things a bit calling them friends. I think Connie likes me just fine, but I'm not sure she trusts me. I am positive Katie neither likes nor trusts me. We have a history. It's a long story and I look bad at the end. But that didn't stop me.

"Hey, mind if I sit with you two?" I said with what I was sure was the furthest thing from the phony smile Cash had given me. I'd practiced in the mirror. Smiles that are both big and genuine take effort, and I'd wanted to make sure that when I finally got around to talking to Tina, I had the right look on my face. Friendly, but not frantic. Confident, but not smug. It takes work to hit that perfect balance.

"Sure." Connie moved her books so I could sit across from them. Katie said nothing, but at least she didn't dump her enchilada on my lap. I took that as progress.

11

"I need a woman's point of view," I told them.

Connie blushed. Katie glared at me.

"Have you met the new guy?" I rolled my eyes in Cash's direction. Connie blushed deeper and Katie nodded. "What do you think of him, guy-wise? I mean, is he the kind of guy who rocks your world?"

"Why?" Katie asked, suspicion oozing from every pore of her body.

"I'm interested in learning what girls find attractive. Especially girls like you." Flattery is a good technique for getting information from someone.

"Oh." Katie looked confused. She hasn't been uncertain about anything since before potty training, so I felt a tiny thrill at bamboozling her.

Connie looked thoughtful. "He's very good-looking."

"Girls like that?"

"Sure, but it's not everything."

"What else do you look for?"

"Personality." Katie was staring at me with an odd expression that I couldn't understand, but I liked her answer; I am Mr. Personality.

"Cool. What—" The bell rang before I could ask any more questions, and everyone started hurrying out of the cafeteria. I watched Tina and Cash walk down the hall together as I headed toward my next class.

Clearly, I'd been panicking in the clutch just because I didn't have enough information about romance. Once I collected enough data, I'd make Tina forget all about that guy and his straight teeth and perfect hair and big shoulders.

I just had to figure out how to figure out girls.

Guys have been getting girls to fall in love with them for millions of years. My only problem was that I'd never applied myself before. But that was about to change. Big-time.

2

The Scientific Mind Believes that Observing the Behavior of Test Subjects Is Essential

I was sitting in class after lunch pretending to pay attention, but really I was planning my next move.

Love is about chemistry, right? Chemistry is science.

I'd been reading a copy of *The Structure of Scientific Revolutions* I'd found in our basement. It's a classic, I guess. Good thing Mom's old schoolbook was highlighted so I could skip around and only read the important parts. I'd never have been able to make sense of it otherwise.

I was reading it because I was going to take a scientific approach to matters of the heart. I'd apply the principles of forming a hypothesis, then research, study, observe and experiment to understand the chemistry between males and females. Empirical, objective and systematic data collection and analysis and the study of culture and society would help me figure out this girl thing. Sounds complicated, but it's just a fancy way to say I was going to do some girl-watching.

If I wanted to unleash my inner Casanova, I'd have to tap into my inner, umm, Copernicus. Or some genius like him.

The simplest route, of course, would be to ask Tina out and see what happened. But only the foolish scientist experiments on himself; look at the tragedy of Madame Curie, who was poisoned and actually died after testing radiation on herself. Men and women of science who know their history study subjects other than themselves in order to achieve a clear-eyed perspective. Not to mention results that don't injure or kill them.

I needed to observe someone close by. Where to start?

Aha! My parents.

I know there's nothing romantic about any-body's parents. But clinically speaking, they've been married for . . . wow, I'm fourteen, Daniel's fifteen and Sarah's sixteen, so, um, forever. They'd be an excellent home lab launch.

I flipped open a notebook and started listing what I knew about my parents and their relationship, because the science book had said: "Knowing the rules and standards of a preexisting situation is imperative."

Here are Rules of the Spencer House as I've noticed them:

(1) Don't mess with Mom after a long day at the bookstore.

(2) Don't mess with Dad after a bad day on the golf course.

Interesting corollary: Mom's hobbies never make her crabby, and Dad leaves his troubles at the office.

Okay, find out what blisters Tina's behind and then don't do that.

I was off to an excellent start.

(3) When they argue, Mom always says the same thing: "You *hear* me, but you never *listen*." Dad looks as confused as I feel when she says that. Listen, hear, what's the difference?

So, listen to Tina *and* hear what she's saying. Or at least look very intense and nod a lot.

(4) Mom and Dad are happiest if their favorite food is involved. Mom relaxes when she has a stash of chocolate peanut butter candies, and Dad gets mellow after deep-dish pizza.

Ergo, find out Tina's favorite food. Hope it's something simple like burgers, not weird like those hairy little kiwi fruits.

In summation: Don't annoy her, listen—and hear—her, and feed her. Except for the listening/hearing part, it's kind of like having another cat. And I am an excellent pet owner.

But then it struck me that my parents are nothing like me and Tina. I needed more information about male-female interaction than what I'd seen. I needed to watch my parents on a date. The trouble was, I was pretty sure my dad hadn't asked my mom out on a date in seventeen years, and if I suggested it to him, he'd think I was bonkers.

I was stuck until I decided I'd set up a surprise date for them at home that I could observe.

I'm brilliant.

I really am.

I spent the rest of the school day planning everything.

After school, I dipped into my savings from

both my jobs and stopped at the grocery store for supplies. I had a sense that creating the right atmosphere was important to the perfect date. I got floor cleaner out from under the sink and stepped on two wads of paper towels. Then I sprayed and shuffled over the stickier, grimier parts of the kitchen floor until the parts that the overhead light fell on shone clean. Good enough. I walked through every room spritzing Springtime Fresh deodorizer and I cleaned the cat box, even though it was in the laundry room in the basement and not likely to stink up the living room. No one had remembered to do this for at least a thousand evacuations. Poor kitty.

I ran around the entire house with a laundry basket, picking up books, dirty mugs, empty chip bags, old newspapers, piles of mail, shoes, socks, jackets, sweaters, phone chargers and wet towels. I shoved the basket in the garage. I'd deal with all that stuff later. Or never.

Just as I was coming back into the kitchen from the garage, the doorbell rang.

"Hi, Dutchdeefuddy. You forgot about babysitting me."

It was Markie, my preschool neighbor. His mother was in the car, and she waved goodbye as she zoomed down the driveway. Markie's parents had recently decided to get a divorce, and they think I'm a good influence on him. Markie's a great kid, but I understand his mom's relief at getting away. He's high-maintenance. He's curious and he has a lot to say, about everything—he kind of sounds like the inside of my head, which is probably why we get along so well. He makes up words when he doesn't have the right ones, like *dutchdeefuddy*, which means "best most favorite buddy in the world forever."

I was just as glad he was there, though, because I had to get dinner on the table and I needed a sous-chef. "C'mon, Markie, you can help me make a special dinner for my parents." He flashed me a thumbs-up and headed to the drawer in the kitchen where we'd put an apron for him when he helped me bake cookies awhile back.

"What're we making?" He was all business, pushing the little step stool over to the counter where I had laid out all our supplies and rolling up his sleeves. He didn't wash his hands, but then again neither did I.

"Spaghetti."

"I love sketti. It's like eating warm white worms. 'Cept they don't wiggle in your mouth like the brown ones. In the yard."

"Well, sure, but what I really like is how easy it is. Any idiot can boil water."

He nodded like he spent a lot of time worrying about preparing meals.

"Oh," I said, "and don't eat any more worms from the yard; that can't be good for you. Okay?"

Markie shrugged, clearly reluctant to make any promises.

"We're going to serve baby carrots as our vegetable because I don't like salad." I pulled a serving bowl out of the cabinet.

Markie scrunched up his face and gagged in support.

"I also got crescent rolls in a tube because food that comes from a tube is genius." I slammed the container on the side of the countertop and the seal broke, oozing out soon-to-be rolls. Markie clapped for the sound and visual effects. "Here, you can roll up the little triangles—see, here's how—and put them on the pan while I get the spaghetti started."

A few minutes later, after I'd struggled to open the sauce jar and measured out the spaghetti into the boiling water, I turned back to Markie and the pan of mushy dough blobs. I'm optimistic by nature, but there was no way anything that shape was going to bake into anything even remotely like little crescents. Maybe we'd invented a new culinary trend—bread nuggets. Oh well, nothing a big slather of butter wouldn't help. I put the butter dish on the dining room table and then, just to be sure, I melted some in a small bowl and gave Markie a brush to paint the gooey roll-like entities.

"Markie, everything tastes better brushed with melted butter." Besides, my parents would be dining by candlelight, and with any luck, they wouldn't have a clear visual on what was in front of them.

"Hey—dessert?" Markie asked. "Dinner has dessert. If it doesn't, it's lunch."

"Good point. I'm on it. You might not know this, but romantic dinners require more than one dessert—that's how you know it's not just another dinner. So I bought fresh strawberries to dip in melted chocolate. And we're also making cookies from a tube because that goes with the rolls in a tube. I looked for a main course in a tube, but that's not invented yet."

"Bummer."

We wound up eating more of the raw cookie dough than we got on the pan, and I kicked myself when the sugar rush made Markie hyper. But then

I remembered something I'd seen at the movies and handed Markie the bunch of roses I'd bought at the grocery store when I'd been buying food. Generally, the kid breaks everything and leaves a trail of crap behind him as wide as a migrating herd of buffalo, so scattering rose petals was the perfect job for him. Plus he got to burn off some energy running through the house, singing and flinging petals.

He's a tough little booger, didn't complain about the thorns, except for: "Hey, you didn't tell me these flowers bite!"

"They're part tiger."

He growled at me, tossed another handful of petals and dashed out of the kitchen again, still singing. A singing child is a happy child. I don't know if I read that somewhere or made it up, but it makes sense to me.

Man, if I'm half as good at romance as I am at child care, Tina won't know what hit her.

The oven timer dinged and I took the food-item-formerly-known-as-crescent-rolls and the cookies out of the oven. I inspected them. Not too burned to eat. So I scraped them onto serving plates. I stirred the simmering sauce and poked at the boiling pasta and called Markie to help me determine if

22

the spaghetti was fully cooked. I scooped a tongful of noodles into a bowl and let Markie hurl them at the refrigerator to see if they stuck. I couldn't remember if you wanted them to stick or slide to the floor, so I was happy that we seemed to have a 50-50 thing going. I drained the rest of the noodles, dumped them in a bowl and poured the bubbling sauce into a gravy boat. If I had things my way, we'd use a gravy boat at every meal.

"Food is always better if you can pour stuff on it—ketchup, melted cheese, chocolate sauce," I said to Markie. Might as well give the kid some essential culinary information. Kids on my watch leave with valuable information and important life lessons under their belt. I don't even charge extra for the enriched educational experience.

I carried the food to the dining room while Markie set the table. He put three spoons and no knives at every place setting, even though I told him only two people were going to be eating dinner and they could be trusted with butter knives and forks. He looked skeptical. With kids, you have to pick your battles, so three spoons it was. I lit the candles.

We studied our work.

Everything looked exactly like I'd planned it,

except for the silverware. Plus, it was perfect timing. My folks should be home from work in a few minutes; my big brother, Daniel, had hockey practice; my sister, Sarah, was at work; and Mom and Dad would assume I was over at Markie's and they had the house to themselves. Monday just happens to be the only day of the week they always get home at the same time. The gods of love were smiling on me. My parents were walking into a love shack and didn't even realize it.

I heard their cars pull into the garage. I grabbed Markie by the back of his shirt, yanking him off his feet, and carried him under my arm like a football, hitting the stereo's On button for the mood music as I hurtled past and ducked into the coat closet near the front door.

Once we were both crouched inside the closet with the door shut, I gave Markie my portable DVD player and earphones to keep him occupied—and silent—while I made my observations. I didn't have any kiddie movies, so I slipped in *Animals of the Serengeti*. Markie's eyes widened as the camera panned over the desert and the stampeding herd of wildebeests. Good choice, Kev! The kid'll learn some fun facts about wild animals in Africa, as well as the principles of scientific research.

I clutched a pad of paper and a pen for notes. Through the slats in the closet door, I had a view of the living room and the dining room, and I was ready to have my parents teach me all there was to know about romance.

We heard a key in the front door.

I handed Markie a banana and peeled one for myself. Quiet food for purposes of observation. And bananas are brain food.

The door opened and my parents stepped into the house.

"Why are these rose petals all over my living room floor?" Mom dropped to her hands and knees and started crawling after the trail of petals, picking them up and examining the carpet for damage. "You have no idea how much it's going to cost to have those stains steam-cleaned out of the carpet."

"The cat is sitting in a bowl of spaghetti on the dining room table!" Dad yelled.

Oh. Well. I could congratulate myself on the forethought I'd shown in not pouring sauce over the noodles. Furry noodles were gross, but a tomato-covered feline streaking around the house would have been worse than flower stains on the carpet.

Dad made a grab for the cat, who sprang out of the serving dish, knocking it to the floor and tipping over the candles. From the closet, I watched the candles set the basket of buttery bread nuggets on fire.

Dad grabbed one of Mom's good linen napkins to beat out the small fire. But the rolls were more kindling than carbs, and Dad's fanning action fed the flames and set the napkin on fire. Things got kind of scary for a second, especially when he slipped and fell flat on his back on some noodles, a smoldering napkin in his hand. He struggled to his feet, grabbed the water pitcher I'd set near his place and dumped ice water all over the table.

"What's going on in here?" Mom was standing in the doorway, clutching two fistfuls of smushed rose petals, watching my father ruin all my hard work.

"I was trying to put out the fire the cat started."

"There is no possible response to that statement."

Dad shrugged and gathered the corners of the tablecloth like he was trying to contain and lift the mess.

"That is my grandmother's antique linen table-cloth! Don't even think of using it like a drop cloth."

Dad shook his head but looked confused.

"Go get me a trash bag from the kitchen"—Mom pushed the petals into his hand—"and throw these away. I'll start picking through this disaster."

Teamwork. My parents were clearly demonstrating the key ingredient in any successful relationship—working together through a crisis. In a strange and frightening way, this date was turning out even better and more informative than I'd planned. Markie, who had been fast-forwarding through the documentary—the kid has the attention span of a hummingbird—whispered, "Oh no, the hyena is swallowing a whole baby pig."

"Do we have any antihithtamine?" I heard my father call from the kitchen. "I think the thrawberrieth I juth ate are making my tongue ith. Thee, I can't thpeak clearly. Dothe my thkin look thplothy?"

Oops. I'd forgotten Dad was allergic to strawberries. My bad, but then again, I'm only fourteen; what was Dad's excuse for eating berries in the first place?

Just then the kitchen smoke detector set off a

horrible whining screech. If there are tormented souls wailing in Hell, this is what they sound like.

"I'll open windowth," Dad hollered over the noise. "Where ith all thith thmoke coming from? Who did thith?"

"Ouch!" I heard my mother yell as a pan dropped. "The burner was still on! One of my best pots got scorched. And what the . . . the oven is still on too, and"—she coughed twice—"something . . . turned into smoking ash on the bottom."

I'd thought a few rolls might have tumbled off the baking sheet when I took them out of the oven. I'm a little bit chicken about burning myself so I always move really fast near the oven, and there are usually some food casualties. It's not like me to leave appliances on, though; I'm very conscientious.

Hey! I couldn't see my parents in the kitchen. But I could hear; it wasn't hard to imagine the scene.

"Here, take two of these and drink some water. You'll be fine." Mom must have handed Dad allergy pills and turned her attention back to the mess. She's not the most sympathetic person I ever met. "What *is* all this? I left a perfectly clean kitchen this morning and came home to a room full of dirty dishes and a small fire on my dining room table and billowing smoke everywhere."

"Tharah and Daniel and Kevin all had planth after thchool," Dad said. "Do you think dinner fairieth cooked for uth?"

"I like the way you leap to the most logical conclusion, Michael, but no, I doubt that's a reasonable explanation. Maybe it was Buzz?"

"No, your thithter thayth cooking maketh her nervouth and thath why eating out wath invented."

"Look at this mess." Even from the closet I could hear Mom sigh as she moved between the wreck of the dining room table and the disaster that was the kitchen. I had meant to clean up everything later, while they were supposed to be sitting at the table, staring into each other's eyes.

"I didn't even know we had thith many panth and ditheth," Dad said.

I was trying to figure out if I should (a) stay in the closet and keep observing, (b) sneak out of the closet, the house and the neighborhood, move to another state and pretend I had nothing to do with this catastrophe or (c) emerge, claim responsibility and take over cleaning duties, when Markie exploded right next to me like a flock of ducks after the first shot.

He leapt to his feet, sobbing, flew screeching out of the closet and zoomed into the kitchen, waving his arms and screaming.

"What is going on here?" Mom scooped him up, sat at the kitchen table, and started cooing comforting words to him.

I answered from the doorway: "Apparently, I should have taken into consideration the suggestion on the box that this film was not recommended for children under twelve."

"What film?"

"The horrible one where baby animals get eaten," Markie sniffled. What a wuss, I thought.

"Why did you let him watch something like that?" Mom glared at me.

"So we could hide in the closet and spy on you," Markie answered for me, although not with the word choice I'd have selected.

Mom patted him and stared at me in shock.

"Why were you thpying on uth?" Dad asked.

"I wasn't spying, I was observing. I made dinner and everything."

"By 'and everything' I assume you did not intend the mess, the fire and the hysterical preschooler," Mom said.

"Well, no, not those parts." Who did she think would *plan* something like that? I turned to Markie: "You don't feel permanently scarred, do you, big guy?" He shook his head.

"What *wath* all thith? In the planning thtageth, that ith?" Dad looked around at the disaster.

"I was trying to set up a romantic date for you two."

"Why on earth would you do that?"

"I want to learn more about romance. Strictly through observation, of course. Eventually, I'd like to experience it myself. I arranged a romantic date for you so I could watch and learn."

My parents gave each other a look that even Teddy the cat could read: *You* take this one. I saved them both the trouble and jumped back into data collection mode. "What's the most romantic thing you can say about each other?"

I started cleaning up, hoping to impress them with my industriousness, and Markie snuggled into my mother's lap. Good thinking, little one, I said to myself; moms are always more calm and reasonable when someone small is cuddling them.

"Even after all these years, he still puts the toilet seat down," Mom said, looking happier than I would have guessed the memory of such a gesture would make a person.

"That doesn't sound like much."

"It does if your bare butt has ever been plunked into the toilet bowl in the middle of the night."

"I see your point. Dad?"

"Oh, my turn, uh, give me a thecond here, um . . . I can't dethide whith element of your mother ith motht thpecial and, uh . . ." I swear he was breaking out in a sweat. Either that or he was having a secondary allergic reaction to the strawberries.

"I never ask him what the most romantic thing about our relationship is," Mom said. And she answers the tricky questions for him, too.

Dad looked relieved that he didn't have to come up with anything. Mom looked hungry. Neither one of them looked madly in love with the other.

It's official: there is no romance in this house. My folks are very practical people. But the last time I'd meddled in my parents' marriage, they wound up in couples' counseling. So I guess you could count this date and Q&A session as a success.

For a guy with my track record.

3

The Scientific Mind Appreciates Historical Data and the Contemporary Scene

Clearly, happy marriages are worthless in terms of edification for the young.

I needed to study someone with lots of experience: Auntie Buzz and her 3.5 marriages.

Auntie Buzz is my mother's younger sister and she lives in the studio apartment over our garage. She owns an interior decorating company and she mainlines caffeine, hence the nickname. She has had three marriages and three divorces, plus one spring break fling that may or may not have been legal south of the border. Auntie Buzz is savvy in the ways of the heart. Just who I needed to consult.

Markie and I headed over to Buzz's place after we

finished de-noodling the refrigerator and the dining room floor. Markie's a quick study—he insisted on pouring cereal into bowls for my parents for their dinner to make up for the fire and the smoke and the mess—and he showed them how to crumble the unburned parts of the cookies and mix them with vanilla ice cream for a dessert that was allergy-free.

As we left the house, I looked back over my shoulder and saw Mom and Dad standing together at the kitchen counter, eating cereal and catching each other up on their day. Perfectly content. There's no accounting for taste, I guess, but when Tina and I are adults and married, things will be different. I'm the kind of person who'll make happily ever after rock.

If I can just nail that all-important first date.

"Enter at your peril," Buzz called when Markie knocked on her apartment door.

Markie ran in. "Can I play on your computer?"

"Sure. Here, you can finish decorating the room I was working on. Maybe you can help me find a way to make a guest room fresh and exciting." Buzz got Markie settled in front of the computer on her kitchen table and showed him how to click and drag furniture into the empty space.

"I'm going to put chairs all over so you can jump and jump and never touch the floor!" he said, pounding on the keys.

"Sounds fresh and exciting to me." I turned to Buzz, who was pouring coffee into a mug big enough to hold a Pomeranian. For Auntie Buzz, caffeine is a primary food group. She wrinkled her nose and sniffed as she sat next to me at the kitchen table.

"You smell like you've been sitting in a barbecue pit," she said. "What's up?"

"Cooking mishap."

"Ah. Been there, done that, have the incident report from the fire department. What brings you over? I know it's not cooking lessons."

"I need you to tell me how to win a woman's heart."

"Why?"

"I'm collecting data on male-female relationships."

"Because . . ."

"I'm lacking in know-how."

"That never stopped anyone before. The Earth's population is something like seven billion right now, and I doubt any one of those people possessed suitable info before repopulating their home planet."

"I want to do things the right way."

"That'd be a first."

"I just want to go on a date! Not . . . repopulate."

"Smart. Especially at your age."

"Can I ask you some questions about your experience in the romance department?"

"I'm probably the last person you should be asking questions like that, but sure, go ahead."

"How'd you know he was the One?"

"Which one?"

"All of them. In order."

"First time, I was young and stupid. Then, not so young and still stupid. Finally, I was not so young and *very* stupid."

"That's depressing."

"The beginnings were always fun."

"Were you nervous? Did they fall down? Did you like them right away or did it come to you gradually? What did they say—exactly—to get you to go out on a date with them? How much do looks count? How important is a good sense of humor? How do you find out what you have in common without feeling like you're interrogating them, kind of like I'm doing to you right now? Do you believe in love at first sight? How young is too young to believe you've found your soul mate? What's the difference between true love and crushing despair?"

"That's a whole lotta wondering. Doesn't your head hurt?"

"You have no idea."

"Did you speak to your parents about all this?"

I snorted and rolled my eyes. "They're anti-romance. No help at all."

"Don't tell them I said this, but that's what I'd have guessed. Between your mother and her books, and your father and his spreadsheets, not to mention you three kids, I can't imagine . . . But"—she looked thoughtful—"they also haven't spent a minute in divorce court, either. So maybe they're on to something."

"Um . . ."

"But we're here to talk about you: I assume there's a special girl who's caught your eye?"

I nodded.

"Have you let her know how you feel?"

"Are you joking?"

"You're scared?"

"I'm petrified. Which is so not like me."

"Girls are scary," Markie said. He had stopped decorating Auntie Buzz's guest room on the computer.

I peeked over his shoulder and saw that he'd filled the space, as promised, with dozens of chairs. And a whirlpool. Good thinking, very restful, your feet stay off the ground at all times and the soothing bubbles whirl away all your stress. "Maisie LeBeau, at preschool? She's mean. She butts in line. If you say anything, like 'Maisie, don't butt,' she pinches your arm. See!" He showed us a black-and-blue mark on his tiny bicep. "Girls are scary."

"Amen." Markie and I exchanged a meaningful look full of male knowledge passed down through generations from father to son and dutchdeefuddy to preschooler. Then he sneezed and sprayed me with wet germs. Moment over.

"Pretend I'm her." Buzz put down her coffee cup as I wiped Markie goo off my face.

"Excuse me?"

"Let's have a conversation, and I'll play her while you practice asking her out. It's good experience, helps work out the kinks in your technique. C'mon, what've you got to lose?"

Even though I knew it was my Auntie Buzz and not really Tina, I still got nervous. My mind started to do that Morse code dot-blip-dash thing with words, and breathing felt like a really complicated

38

procedure, and all my sweat glands decided to show off what they could do, and my tongue felt like it had just been carpeted.

"Uh . . ."

"Okay, I'll start. I assume you go to school together?" I think I nodded, but it might have been more of an involuntary twitch. "Good. Lots of opportunity to run into her. What's her name?"

"T—T—Tuh—Teee-uh-na." Great. My voice cracked. And it wasn't even really Tina.

"All right," Auntie Buzz said. "I'm Tina and you're going to ask me out and . . . scene." She slammed her hands together like a clapper board in the movies, closed her eyes, inhaled deep and slow, held her breath for a second as she rolled her shoulders, and then exhaled as her eyes flew open and she broke into a huge grin. "Hi! Kev! Hey! What's up?"

Auntie Buzz is wasted in interior decorating. She had transformed herself into an eighth-grade girl in front of my very eyes. Not the one I wanted to go out with, but still, it was impressive.

"Tina's not so . . . perky. Can you take it down a notch?"

"Sure. She's laid-back. I get it." Buzz stared down at the floor for a few seconds, took another breath, looked up, batted her eyes and—truth—purred at me. "Kevinnnnnnn. How are youuuuuu?"

"Uh, wow, she's also not quite so . . . sultry. She's only fourteen, you know."

"Fourteen, right." Auntie Buzz looked down at the floor, breathed slowly for quite a long time and finally threw up her hands. "Hmmm. I can do cheery or flirty. I can't find the middle ground."

"Well, um, thanks for, uh, trying."

"No prob."

"What's your best advice?"

"Get a prenup."

"Your best advice for a fourteen-year-old asking a girl out on a first date."

"Right, got ahead of myself. Wow, it's been a long time since your Auntie Buzz was on a first date. Hmmm . . . let me see. Oh, I know: Don't give her a spider."

"I wasn't planning on it. Why would that leap to mind?"

"Denny DeClewit. He asked me out once in high school and then handed me a shoe box with a big, hairy spider in it when he came to the door to pick me up."

"What did you say?"

"I screamed and dropped the box. The spider escaped. We spent an hour on the front porch trying to find it, and he was so mad that as soon as he recaptured the spider, he left. We never did wind up going out."

"That sounds like a terrible date."

"It wasn't my worst."

"What was?"

"When Charlie Jaros and I got arrested."

"Do I even want to know why?"

"Expired tags on his license plate."

"You can get arrested for that?"

"No, but you can for smart-mouthing a cop, which Charlie did. The police officer took us to the station to make the point that when a cop says 'Let me see your title and registration,' he doesn't want to see your membership card for the Intergalactic League of SuperHeroes. Humor is best reserved for after you've gotten the ticket."

"A good lesson."

"Uh-huh. I went on a picnic with Todd Carrier one time and we both got poison oak. He wound up in the emergency room after he suffered a really bad reaction and had trouble breathing. Your grand-parents got fed up sending me on dates and picking me up at the police station and the hospital."

"I bet."

"You're welcome."

"For what?"

"For setting the bar so low with my love life that you can't possibly help but improve on my standards."

"I was kind of hoping for more than that."

"What were you hoping for?"

"Amazing, transcendent love that stands the test of time and inspires people to write love songs, epic poems, movies and plays."

"You're in eighth grade—pace yourself. Start with not crossing state lines in possession of stolen livestock." I raised my eyebrows. "Wally Charles," she said, nodding. "Senior year in high school. Don't ask."

"Can I put a slide from the bedroom to the kitchen?" Markie yelled. "I can't get the clicker-thing to do that."

"Here, control shift F6 overrides the command on this program. While you're at it, put a fire pit in the guest bath. I get chilly toweling off after a shower."

"Can I have a garage-door opener on the closet?"

"I'm only sorry I didn't come up with that myself. What do you think about busting out that exterior wall, adding glass pocket doors and then rolling the bed to the outside patio on rails?"

"Uh . . . What do you think, Dutchdeefuddy?"

"Kiss Auntie Buzz goodbye, Markie, and let's get you home. Thanks for the, um, advice, Buzz."

"Any time, Kev, and bring Markie over more often. He knocked me right out of my creative block." She was parked at her computer, clicking and dragging.

"Then the visit wasn't a total waste."

I don't think she heard me.

4

The Scientific Mind Embraces Experimental Difficulties

Auntie Buzz is nuts. That's a given. And I was nuts to talk to her.

I wasn't going to learn anything practical from her about matters of the heart.

I needed to analyze someone closer to my own age. My sister, Sarah, has been dating Doug for . . . huh, how about that? I don't really know. I don't pay much attention to my sister, and Doug has more in common with a wheelbarrow full of wet cement than a fully functioning human being.

Having entertained, educated, protected and enlightened Markie for a few hours, I took him back to his house and walked home to find Sarah sitting at her desk, doing homework. As usual, she didn't look happy when I popped my head in the door. I can't say I blamed her; I usually drop by to give her a hard time. Sarah and I could use some improvement in our communication skills. No time like the present.

"Hey."

"Hey."

A better start than usual. Even if she couldn't be bothered to look up from her notes.

"How're things going with you and Doug?"

"So you do know his name. I'd been wondering if you thought his parents named him WonderTurd, WeenieKing and DweebBot." She licked her finger and turned a page, silently telling me how bored she was with our conversation.

"Great guy. He gets my sense of humor and knows that nicknames between guys are signs of, uh, respect. So, how's my buddy Doug? How's your relationship?"

This did make Sarah look up from her homework.

"My. Re. La. Tion. Ship."

"Yeah. With Doug. You know, you and Doug. You two getting along, getting serious, feeling committed?"

"Why do you ask?"

45

"Inquiring minds want to know."

"So why would *you* be asking?"

"Ha ha, good one. You're a funny girl." I have no idea how my crabby, nasty, smart-aleck sister landed herself a boyfriend, with her bad attitude and cranky moods. I tried to look at her as a guy looking at a girl, but that made me throw up a little in my mouth. I got back to the conversation. "Seriously, you two seem reasonably happy together. How'd you know he was the one? How'd he know you were the one?"

"What's with the third degree here? It can't be because you care if I'm happy or not."

I'd been afraid of this; I was going to have to tell her the truth.

"I'm thinking about asking a girl out."

"You?" She narrowed her eyes, studying me. Her nose twitched like I smelled bad. "Really? Well, they say there's a lid for every pot, so I guess you've got a chance of meeting someone equally deranged and socially challenged. I wouldn't count on it, though."

I clenched my teeth. This was about the time in our conversations where I'd usually flip her the bird or she'd slam the door in my face. But this evening I was determined to accumulate data.

46

"I appreciate your feedback." I'd read once that this was a good way to defuse an insult. "But more than your feelings about my ability to get a girl-friend, I'm curious to know how you make things work with Doug."

"He's cute. We have mutual friends. He does what I tell him. I let him talk about, um, whatever it is he's interested in. Don't tell him, but sometimes I only pretend to listen."

"That doesn't sound very exciting."

"I didn't want exciting. I was looking for hot."

"Oh."

Sarah did something she'd never done before: she took pity on me. "Look, Kev, don't overthink things. Just be yourself."

"That can't possibly be the best plan."

"Probably not in your case, but you still might give it a try." She paused. "But you should practice first."

"Practice what?"

"Speaking."

"I'm an excellent conversationalist."

"No, you're chatty—there's a difference. Go ahead and tell me something nice about me. Girls like compliments."

I already knew that part, but what the heck, I could use all the rehearsal time I could get. What is it with women and acting? First Buzz, now Sarah. I hoped that Tina, once we started dating, wasn't going to make me run lines with her like this. That could get old real fast.

"You look nice today." I tried to smile as I lied.

"Enhhh!" My sister sounded like a game show buzzer cutting off a contestant with the wrong answer. "No girl wants to be told she looks 'nice.' It's a boring noncompliment that signifies nothing. Be specific. 'Your hair looks phenomenal. Very shiny.' And don't say 'today' or she'll wonder if you thought she looked like crap yesterday."

"Oh. Thanks. Your hair looks phenomenal. Very shiny. What do I do next?"

"Ask her a question about her day. 'How'd you do on that social studies quiz?'"

"Sounds kind of boring. Shouldn't I, um . . . memorize a poem or write her a love letter or give her flowers or . . . serenade her outside her bedroom window?"

"Yeah, sure, if you want her to think you're weird and creepy and might have a collection of dead animal parts in your basement."

"That bad, huh?"

"Trying too hard. Relax. Girls like to know you've been thinking about them, not obsessing."

"Are you sure about all this?"

"I'm a girl, aren't I?"

Before I could even open my mouth, she cut me off and said, "I'm going to call Christine and Rebecca and Carrie and Amie and get them over here to put together a dating boot camp for you. You clearly need more help than one person can provide."

Again, she stopped me from speaking. "Go do something productive for half an hour; I'll call you when the girls get here and we're ready for you."

The smart scientist knows when the odds are against him, so I went to the kitchen and nuked some pizza puffs. It was eight p.m. and, other than the banana in the closet with Markie, I hadn't had any supper. I was on my third plate of puffs when the doorbell rang and Sarah took the stairs in what sounded like a single bound to get to the entryway before I did. She threw open the door and Christine, Rebecca, Carrie and Amie were standing there—her best friends since they were hatched together in the witchbaby nursery. They're exactly like

Sarah, only with four times as much bossy, spoiled, put-Kevin-down attitude. I had a strong feeling this wasn't going to end well.

Sarah herded them toward her room; they peeked at me in the kitchen as they went by. Rebecca rolled her eyes in my direction and Christine, who hasn't acknowledged me since I was seven and barfed on her during a picnic, looked over the top of her glasses at me menacingly. Carrie and Amie, who were whispering and cackling, only glanced at me before disappearing into Sarah's room.

The great scientist Galileo seared his retinas because he stared directly at the sun as he refined the telescope. If he could sacrifice his vision for the sake of astronomy, I could risk a little of my time, and my self-esteem, to listen to my sister's evil coven. And they might have some helpful insights. Stranger things have happened.

I'd finished my puffs and was wondering what could be taking the girls so long when Sarah finally yelled, "Kev!" I took a deep breath and headed to her room. They were sitting on her bed, lined up like a firing squad. Sarah gestured to her desk chair. I sat and faced them. No one offered me a blindfold, though.

"We took a vote: three to two," Sarah said. "We'll give you some advice so you don't make a total fool out of yourself, but mostly so you don't traumatize and ruin the self-confidence and future dating prospects of some unsuspecting girl."

I figured Christine had voted against me. I'd bet that Sarah, my own flesh and blood, was the other dissenter, even though she'd called the meeting. That would be so typical of her.

"First of all, we've agreed you're not completely hideous-looking." Sarah looked at her notes. They'd discussed me and taken notes?

"I can live with that. What next?"

"Personality-wise: two of us think you have the potential to be funny, one person thinks you're half an evolutionary step from being a turtle, and two of us just want to get you paired off so our little sisters aren't in danger of dating you."

"Could be worse. Go on."

"The best thing about you is that you're my brother. And your best friend, JonPaul, is hunky and athletic and popular. You should stress the proximity to me and JonPaul when you talk to this poor girl."

"That way," Rebecca said, "even if she has doubts

51

about you, she'll think she might be missing some-thing because of who you're related to and who you hang with."

"It's vicious and deeply unkind, but it makes sense. Are we almost done?"

"We haven't even started," Sarah said. "Now, moving on to your fashion sense: how do I put this gently?"

"You don't have any and you look like you just left the site of a natural disaster." Christine clearly loved getting her two cents in.

"What's wrong with my clothes?"

Sarah ran her eyes appraisingly up and down my body. "A faded T-shirt from a Buket o' Puke 'n Snot concert and jeans that sag in the butt, with ripped-out knees, don't say 'Your dad will trust me and your best friends will be jealous of you for having landed me.'"

"Okay, fun as it is to be eviscerated by you, let's shift into the Q&A portion. Now, how many of you have a boyfriend?" Only Sarah's hand went up. "Then how are you qualified to give me advice?"

"We're not giving you advice, we're sharing our experiences with you. Four of us don't have boy-friends at the current moment because we chose wrong in the past. We made mistakes that we can help you avoid becoming," Rebecca said.

"Yeah." Carrie jumped in. "And we'd like the chance to mold a guy into something worthwhile. By the time you're our age, guys are pretty much set in their ways. But you're like raw clay, and we could turn you into something . . . well . . . not horrible. We wish some of the older girls had been so considerate of us a few years ago. It would have saved us a lot of wear and tear, I can tell you." Carrie blazed with anger.

"I wish we could get community service hours credit for *this* at school," Sarah grumbled. Sarah tries to turn everything into extra credit or a compensated task. She's very ambitious.

"Well, okay. Thanks for your time and I appreciate your suggestions, but I'm gonna get going now." If I'd been a foot closer to the door—or the window—I'd have thrown myself out of the room.

"You can't go yet; we still have to tell you about all the ways you could inadvertently ruin the mood on a date." Carrie looked panicked.

"And we have a top-ten list of ways loser guys make girls feel weird in the hallway at school."

Amie waved a piece of paper in the air. "Number one: staring at their boobs. Number two: thinking farting is still funny after kindergarten. Number three . . ." I stopped listening.

Man, I thought, if this is what girls in high school are like, I'll just stay in middle school. I'd better get Tina to be my girlfriend quick, before she turns into something like these girls. I slipped out of the room as unobtrusively as possible, but I don't think it mattered: the girls were happily talking about everything that was wrong with guys.

I threw myself on my bed, feeling totally crummy about my dating future, but then I realized that the blame rested with the girls. They were just bitter because they'd had bad experiences. I was lucky—as far as I knew, Tina had never dated anyone else. But I needed to move fast, before Cash got a chance to take her out and be perfect. Or, worse yet, some random guy asked her out and did something stupid, which was starting to sound even easier than I had thought, and ruined guys for Tina forever.

It was going to be hard enough to be an amazing boyfriend without having to live up to Captain Fantastic or make up for some other schlub's mistakes.

5

The Scientific Mind comprehends Variation in Romantic Behavior

Sarah and Doug do not have the kind of relationship I want. If I ever join the army and need to learn how to handle a drill sergeant, I'll be sure to take another look at her.

It was time to consider someone my age, someone more like me, someone happy. I had to find a paradigm worth emulating.

JonPaul and Samantha.

JonPaul's been my best buddy since forever. He's great. Part of the reason we get along so well is because he does every sport known to mankind and a few that have yet to be officially sanctioned so we don't get to spend much time together and we never get on each other's nerves. We'd been hanging out even less the past few weeks because he'd started dating Sam.

I'd spent a fair amount of quality time with Sam myself; she and JonPaul had partnered up with me in a business I invented, ran and shut down in about two weeks' time. Sam was pretty cool. But I'd been so busy with the business that I hadn't really studied them as a couple.

I caught up with JonPaul at his locker before homeroom bell Tuesday morning.

"How'd you get Sam to go out with you?"

"I asked her."

"You just asked her?"

"Yup."

"What'd you say?"

"'Will you go out with me?'"

"That's it? How'd you decide what to say?"

"I wanted her to go out with me. I asked her to."

"Really."

"Yeah. What's up with you?"

"Collecting data. Gathering facts. Analyzing info."

"Cool."

JonPaul almost completely lacks curiosity. That's

one more reason he's so easy to get along with. Me, I might have too much curiosity. It doesn't seem to bother JonPaul, though.

"When's your next date with her?"

"After practice today."

"Can I come?"

"Sure." He dug in his backpack for a protein bar and then looked up at me, suspicion in his eyes. "You don't have any more get-rich-quick plans, do you?"

"No. I'd just like to spend time with you and Sam. Get to know her better. It seems right that I should be better friends with my best buddy's girl."

"Cool."

"What do you do on your dates?"

"Homework mostly, watch TV, eat. We just hang out, it's no big deal."

"And you both like that?"

"Yeah. What's not to like?"

"You don't go fun places and do exciting things?"

"Not really."

"Oh."

Everything I was learning about romance was so ordinary. Where were the butterflies in your gut and the shaking hands and the wanting to build big white Taj Mahals in India to prove your love?

I'd really been hoping for some . . . grand and sweeping gestures. I think big, always have. Maybe actually observing a date in progress would give me a better sense of how everything worked. I could hardly wait for the end of the day to tag along with JonPaul and Sam.

I killed time at the library while JonPaul was at practice.

Tina and Katie walked in together and took over a table for some project they were working on.

Tina smiled and waved, but I pretended I hadn't seen her and tried to look busy, because I wasn't ready to talk to her yet. It was important that the very next time we spoke, I knew what to do and say.

I kept peeking over at her from behind my stack of books, making sure to drop my eyes fast so she wouldn't catch me gawking. I saw Katie studying me a few times, but she'd look back at her books as soon as she saw that I saw her.

I saw Cash, too. He didn't see me. He definitely didn't see me watching him watching Tina. I couldn't tell if Tina noticed he was noticing her. I think Katie saw me scoping out Cash, but I'm not sure.

It was a confusing afternoon, observation-wise.

I was relieved when I could leave all that watching behind and meet up with JonPaul at the locker room door. We walked back to his house. Sam's mom dropped her off as we went up the sidewalk. Their timing was impressive, in synch, proof of mutual devotion.

"Hey."

"Hey."

So much for passionate greetings. Sam smiled at me.

"HeyKevgoodtoseeyou." Sam talks really fast.

"You too."

We headed for the kitchen, where JonPaul dumped trail mix in a bowl and Sam pulled three bottles of vitamin water from the fridge. They unpacked their backpacks at the kitchen table, organizing their books and notes. The room was silent except for JonPaul crunching trail mix as he did math problems and Sam riffling through the pages of her social studies textbook. I sat at the counter and watched. I yawned.

I had to fight the urge to hide in JonPaul's front closet and observe them when they didn't know I was there. Maybe my presence was hindering their natural behavior, date-wise.

"Can I borrow your calculator?" and "Do you have an extra blue pen?" were the only words Jon-Paul and Sam exchanged in the forty-seven minutes they sat at the table together.

Finally, they both finished and Sam pulled a bag of beads from her backpack. "Ibroughtthosenew-beadsyouwanted." JonPaul and Sam shared a love of making jewelry; they'd discovered that when my business collapsed. Now they spent all their free time stringing beads on bendy wire and then selling what they made at weekend art fairs. They'd asked me to go with them, but I was still working at Amalgam-ated Waste Management from twelve-thirty to five p.m. and at the storage facility from five-thirty to nine-thirty p.m. on Saturdays and school holidays. It didn't leave me any free time.

"Awesome."

The three of us went into the living room and sat on the couch. I watched them organize beads into color groups. I fell asleep while they were sepa-rating blues into different piles, and when I woke up, JonPaul and Sam were dozing too. Some date. At least he had his arm around her.

JonPaul's idea of dating was a whole lot like

Markie's preschool's idea of quiet time, only without the duck mats and blankies.

I leaned over, woke JonPaul up and whispered, "How can you tell she's your girlfriend?"

"What do you mean?"

"You don't go out and do fun things, neither of you seems nervous around the other person, and birds don't serenade you with tweeting love songs. What makes you girlfriend and boyfriend?"

"We like each other."

"It can't be that easy."

"Why would it be hard?"

"It just is. Everyone knows that."

"Sam and I don't."

"I think you're doing it wrong."

"Maybe so."

JonPaul never hits below the belt or picks a fight, and he won't even respond if you try to start something with him. His complacency, usually one of his best qualities, was making me crazy.

"You seem a lot like my parents."

"Thanks. Your folks are cool."

What can you do with a guy who doesn't take offense and can't decipher sarcasm?

He smiled at me, rested his cheek on the top of Sam's head and fell asleep again.

I let myself out.

I could do better than this. I had to do better than this. I just wished I knew how. Observation, study and rigorous questioning had been a total bust.

I needed to go from study mode to action.

6

The Scientific Mind Relishes the Mixing of Two Elements

My only conclusion thus far: no one in a relationship had anything helpful to share.

People who had already been part of a couple were worse than useless.

As I walked home from JonPaul's, I thought about how fruitless observing my parents, Auntie Buzz, Sarah and her friends, and JonPaul and Sam had proved to be. I was going to have to up my game from passive observation to aggressive experimentation if I wanted to learn anything valuable.

I needed to watch a relationship from the beginning. I wasn't discovering anything meaningful about how to start a relationship from people who weren't in the same boat I was.

And that was when I thought of my older brother.

Daniel, as far as I knew, had not only never been on a date, even though he's fifteen—he might well have never even noticed a girl. Unless she was holding a puck. Even then, he'd have focused on the black rubber disk and missed the girl entirely. Daniel lives for hockey. I asked him once what was important to him besides being on the team and he said, with a straight face, "Kev, nothing else in the world exists except performing well during the game and leaving it all on the ice during practice sessions and taking care of my gear and watching out for my teammates and listening to what Coach says and warming up and cooling down so I avoid injuries and keeping my grades up so I don't get benched." I was impressed. Typically, conversation from my brother ran along the lines of "You going to eat that last pork chop?"

Now I realized that he needed me to help broaden his interests and add color to his life. Therefore, I was going to find a girl for my brother.

He didn't know it yet, but he'd been crying out for me to set him up on a date.

And then I could watch what happened.

Except he never does anything alone—only as part of the first string of his hockey team. So I was going to have to find six girls, one each for the center, the two wingmen, the two guys on defense and the goalie.

Daniel spends so much time with the guys that it feels like I have six older brothers. And I just happened to have read an article in the newspaper that morning about quadruplets: four sisters—Annabeth, Alexandra, Meghan and McKenna Welsh—who go to the private high school in town. It pays to be curious about the world around you and to be well read in terms of current events, it really does. The Welsh girls are famous in our town—they're championship skaters, and they were about to go to the junior nationals to compete. They already had ice in common with the hockey team. Too bad they were quads and not sextuplets, because I was two girls short. Oh well, they'd have skater girlfriends. I wasn't going to let a little thing like numbers get in my way.

Leap and the net will appear, that's my theory.

I checked the time on my cell phone—seven o'clock. Perfect. The hockey team and the Welsh sisters would be practicing. I knew that because skaters are always practicing. They must get withdrawal symptoms if they're off the ice for too long—if they can feel their toes again, they know it's time to get back in their skates. I sent a quick text to my mother, "was @ JPs going 2 rink now did my hmwrk home l8er." Good communication skills are essential in a healthy family unit. Then I turned my matchmaking feet toward the rink.

Before Daniel and I got old enough to be on our own after school, I practically lived at the rink. So I knew that the hockey team would be practicing on the NHL ice and the figure skaters would have the Olympic ice on the other side of the lobby.

I also knew that most likely, the team and the girls hadn't crossed paths. Everyone's very focused during their ice time. They should be—it's really expensive and they guard it with their lives. I've seen them tapping their blades impatiently when they've felt that the Zamboni driver was making new ice too slowly and eating into their allotted time. So each group probably didn't know that the other group existed. It was up to me to change that.

I grabbed a slice of pizza and a soda at the snack bar and headed to the bleachers overlooking the Oly rink. I picked out the Welsh girls easily—they were the prettiest skaters, the highest jumpers, the fastest spinners. Every so often they'd huddle up next to the boards, queuing their program music for the CD player. I noticed they were chummy with two girls in matching warm-up jackets. Perfect. Here were my six girls. I just had to find out who they were, which Welsh girl was which and how I was going to get them to go out with the hockey team.

"Hey, Kevin, long time no see, buddy." Patrick, the rink manager, walked up. "Where you been keeping yourself, and when can we get you on a hockey team like your brother?"

"Pat, good to see you. It's been a while. Hey, who are the girls in the purple jackets?" I pointed.

"Kris and Carol Connor, they looked really good at regionals. Nice girls. Their parents are never late with contracts and checks. I like that in people."

"Yeah, I bet. Hey, I read about the Welsh girls— them going to junior nationals must be good PR for the rink, huh?"

Patrick smiled and turned to study them on the ice.

"Which one is which?" I asked.

"It's like the twisty ties on a bread wrapper."

"Pardon?" How many pucks to the head had Patrick taken over the years?

"If you look at the twisty tie on a loaf of bread at the store, you can tell which day it hit the shelves. Monday is blue, Tuesday is green, Thursday is red, Friday is white and Saturday is yellow."

"Uh-huh."

"The colors are alphabetical, in order of the days of the week they're delivered."

"And you know this because . . ."

"I like fresh bread."

"And this applies to the Welsh girls how?"

"Alexandra is blue, Annabeth is pink, McKenna is purple and Meghan is red. Alphabetical by name *and* color. Brilliant, isn't it?"

"I guess."

"Okay, gotta go, Kev, you let me know when you're ready to get on a team and I'll make it happen."

"You bet." I'd tried hockey once when I was five. Fell down in all my gear. Couldn't get up. Felt like a turtle. Got skated over by peewees screaming for blood. Decided other sports were for me. Like bull-fighting or storm chasing, things that aren't as dangerous and scary.

The Zamboni chugged onto the ice just then, and all the skaters glided off to huddle around tables in the lobby, gulping water and chewing protein bars. The Welsh girls had a table to themselves, and I headed over to make their lives richer and more fulfilling. If I could only think of how to explain my plan for them to date the hockey team without sounding deranged.

"Hey, aren't you Sarah Spencer's brother?" Blue jacket. Alexandra.

"Yeah." She looked happier asking the question than I did answering it.

"We met when I was over at your house a few months ago. Sarah and I volunteer at the hospital together."

"Oh, sure, of course." I didn't have a clue what she was talking about. "I swung by the rink on my way home to congratulate you and your sisters on making it to junior nationals and to wish you luck."

"That's the sweetest thing," Alexandra said.

"I can't believe you did that," Pink Jacket, Annabeth, said.

"Aren't you a nice guy." Purple Jacket. McKenna.

"Wow, thanks, we're really nervous." Red Jacket. Meghan.

I had to take a step back from the barrage of answers. And color.

"Oh well, uh, sure, no problem."

"And you must be thrilled that your brother's team made it to the final round of play-offs."

They did? I wondered when that had happened.

"Oh yeah," I said. "The whole family's . . . um, giddy about it." I was sure some family was, just not mine, but details like that wouldn't help my plan. "In fact, we're having a little celebration this evening. Nothing fancy, just uh . . . light refreshments. The family and Daniel's team and all that. How about you girls stop by after practice? And bring the Connor sisters too."

"You really are the nicest guy," Red Jacket said, "to include them in honor of their good showing at regionals."

"We'll be there. Thanks a lot!" Pink Jacket.

"Can we bring anything?" Purple Jacket.

Other than everything, you mean? "No, of course not. Just yourselves. And the Connor sisters.

Six girls. Six hardworking, successful skating girls. That'd be perfect."

"We skate for another hour and then we'll head over, okay? I remember where you live," Alexandra said.

"See you then," I told them, crossing my fingers they'd still be wearing their identifying warm-up jackets when they arrived, and I jogged across the lobby to the other ice. I spotted Daniel, put two fingers in my mouth and gave an earsplitting whistle. He skated over, backwards because Daniel is such a show-off on skates.

"Kev. What's up?"

"What's up? What's up, he asks! Only congratulations for um, for . . ." Dang, what had she said? Winning, placing, advancing? I really had to start paying better attention to my family. Maybe we could post announcements on the fridge once a week. "Uh, you know, congrats, man, for everything."

"Thanks. We're pretty stoked."

"Mom says to be sure to get the guys to our house by nine for the celebration."

"What celebration?"

"The celebration in, uh, celebration of, uh, the thing."

"Oh yeah, right. Okay, we'll be there after the scrimmage. Will there be food?"

"Will. There. Be. Food. Of course there's going to be food. Look, bro, I gotta motor. Catch you at home."

"At the celebration." Daniel looked really happy and skated back to his buddies. I heard them cheer when he told them about coming over.

It's a good thing that I am a very social person, that I think on my feet and that I do not panic under pressure.

As I left the rink, I speed-dialed my dad.

"Papa Bear here. Speak, youngest cub." My dad is so lame. But I needed his help, so I played along. A little.

"Roar. Look, Dad, can you come get me at the rink? Better yet, I'll start walking and you drive toward me and we'll meet on the road—that'll save time. And then can you take me to the grocery store and buy chips and soda and maybe a cake? Or three?"

"Do I even want to know what this odd request is in service of?" Dad's been around when some of my other plans have hit the fan, so I can't blame him for his suspicion.

"Can you do it?"

"I'm on my way."

"Thanks, Dad."

"But I expect an explanation when I get there."

"No sweat." I actually meant that. On my way out of the lobby to the parking lot, I saw some fluorescent-green flyers congratulating my brother's team for advancing to the final round of the divisional championship series. Dad would be so proud. He wouldn't know what it meant, either, but he'd be proud. Dad is like that.

I handed the flyer to him after we spotted each other on the street and I hurtled across the tarmac and flung myself into the front seat. I explained that soon our house would be overridden with hungry divisional championship hockey players and junior national–bound figure skaters, as well as two girls who had placed well in regionals but were still deserving of light refreshments. As predicted, he was a great sport, and he did spring for the snacks. The pastry gods were with me, because there were two sheet cakes in the grocer's bakery department. One said "Congradulacions" and the other one had a Barbie on it. But I wasn't fussy and I knew the hockey team and skaters wouldn't be picky about free cake.

We stocked up on soda, chips, pretzels, ice cream and a veggie tray the size of a twin bed.

"Mom's working late and Sarah's at Carrie's studying for a test," Dad told me as we were putting all the snacks on the kitchen counter. If I hadn't known better, I'd have sworn this celebration looked planned.

The hockey players and skaters started arriving, and after congratulating them "for, uh, everything. Good job, guys. And, uh, ladies, well done," Dad headed to the basement with his briefcase and a chunk of cake.

The Welsh girls had their warm-up jackets on and the Connor girls had their names embroidered on theirs. So I handed them cups of soda and introduced everybody.

Then I sat back and watched. They mingled. Chatted. Mutual congratulations flew as the cakes shrank on the platters. I stood off to the side and watched things fall into place.

Finally.

At last, I was gleaning some meaningful information from observing guys and girls together. I heard giggles and saw hair tosses, I watched guys suck in their guts and stand up straight, I smelled love—and frosting—in the air. It was a magical thing. I felt tingly all over. Success. About time.

But then again, I've found that hockey players and skaters are very hardworking and eager to please. Their coaches can be fierce—no surprise, given they have knife blades on the soles of their feet—so skaters get good at figuring out what's expected and living up to those standards.

I went to bed happy. Finally, I'd observed a favorable outcome to an experiment.

7

The Scientific Mind
Studies Truth vs. Theories

I'd learned a lot from setting Daniel and his team-mates up on Tuesday night. But on Wednesday I was struggling with a fact that every good scientist knows: results only count if you can replicate them. I needed another test subject.

I also needed to take my mind off the fact that I wanted to punch Cash Devine in the gut and then bury him under twenty cubic tons of waste at the Amalgamated Waste Management site.

I'd arrived at the cafeteria in a good mood. Until I'd looked up from my tuna noodle casserole and had seen Cash reach over and fix Tina's hair. Tina's hair is flawless, there's not a single strand that ever needs adjusting; he was just using that as an excuse to touch her.

I turned away from Cash and my mental images of him covered in coffee grounds, snotty tissues and used cat litter, and thought hard about my next romantic experiment.

Goober!

It'd have to be a blind date, though; no way was I going to convince any girl who'd actually met Goober to go out with him. Good, I was adding challenge to the task. That was smart.

Goober is JonPaul's cousin, a student at the local college. I guess you can call him a student, since he lives on campus and his parents pay tuition; I'm not so sure he qualifies as a student if you think about the scholarly part. He's . . . kind of light in the intellect department. And the hygiene department. And the quick-on-the-uptake department.

But he's a guy and he's single, and as soon as I was on my way home from school on Wednesday, I called him.

"So, Goob, how's the love life?" Best to get right to the matter at hand.

"Bummer, man, none of the chicks on this campus appreciate the Goob."

"Shocking. I might be able to help with that. You busy right now?"

"No, little dude, I've got class, uh, science, social studies, psychology—something—but I can blow it off."

"Okay, come on over, and bring an open mind."

"On my way."

I was eager to find out what Goober was looking for in a girl. I'm not sure why I bothered; I didn't have that many candidates in mind. Or any.

I was waiting for him on the front step when he ambled up the sidewalk.

"Who's the fox?" he whispered as we passed the kitchen on the way to my room.

"What fox?"

"The chick with the books."

"That's my *mother*."

"An older woman. Goober likes."

"No, Goober doesn't like. What's wrong with you? She's my *mother*, she lives here, she's not here to meet you, you moron."

"She available?"

"No! Stop looking at her like that, because you're creeping me out, not to mention offending

her and the sanctity of my entire family structure."
I dragged him to my bedroom and stood between
him and the door to protect Mom. I also sent her
a silent message: LEAVE THE HOUSE IMMEDIATELY. I
made a mental note that our family should do some
work on developing our extrasensory perception. It
would be really helpful to add that to our collective
skill set.

"Sorry, dude. You said to keep an open mind; I
thought maybe you meant you were going to hook
me up with an old lady."

"She's not an old lady, and we're not talking
about her anymore. We're here to talk about what
you find desirable in the opposite sex."

"I'm telling you, your mom checks all the boxes
on Goober's list."

"And I'm telling you: I'm going to punch you in
the head and tell my father, who will also punch you
in the head, if you keep talking about my mother
that way." I took a deep breath. "You need to focus
on why you're here and what I can do for you. I
want to know what kind of girl you're looking for.
Let's start with physical attributes: do you like tall
girls or petite ones?"

"Depends."

"On what?"

"On whether she's hot or not."

"Okay. Define 'hot.'"

He made a gesture with his hands that prompted me to jot down *curvy* in my notes. I nodded professionally, hoping to move this along. "That's a start. Hair color?"

"Nah, man, as long as she's stack—"

"Right, no preference on hair or height, got it. Let's move on from the physical and get to the intellectual." I took another look at Goober and scratched that off my list. "Uh, yeah, okay, never mind that—what about hobbies and interests?"

Goober perked up. "NASCAR, hunting, heavy metal rock bands, video games, extreme bike tricks, ice fishing, greyhound racing, muscle cars and kung fu movies."

"Um, not so much."

"What's wrong with all that stuff?"

"Nothing. You're just not in touch with your feminine side, the kind of things girls like. Like, um, walks on the beach and going out to dinner and visiting museums."

"Nope."

"Which might be part of the reason you're still single. Could you *try* some new things if it got you a date with a hot girl?"

"Yeah . . . I guess . . . but you're gonna hook me up with someone who'll do the kinds of things I like too, right?"

"Relationships," I said as if I knew what I was talking about, "are about compromise. You give a little, she gives a little. You'll see—you just have to be flexible and you'll be surprised at what a great time you have."

"Yeah, maybe. Okay, look: how about if I *com-pro-mise*"—I could tell this was probably Goober's first time using that word—"on the hobby thing but you make sure she's really hot."

"We'll see about that." I wasn't about to promise anything. In fact, the more Goober spoke, the less I felt I could fix him up with anyone.

I sent him away so I could think. A little Goober goes a long way, and I wasn't going to be able to sell him as a great date if I spent much more time with him.

I racked my brain trying to think of the right

girl, and then, out of the blue, the perfect idea came to me. It was what scientists call deductive reasoning. And what I call a stroke of genius.

Betsy Putnam.

The nicest girl I know. She's in college too, and lives a couple of houses down. She was home from school for her grandparents' fiftieth wedding anniversary party—I knew because our family was invited. Betsy volunteered at the library all through high school and was voted most popular, most likely to succeed, homecoming queen and prettiest smile. Her part-time job is giving skating lessons to special-needs kids, so someone like Goober might not seem like such a challenge to her—she's very patient and understanding. And she's so popular that I wouldn't, as Sarah and her friends warned me, "traumatize" her by setting her up with Goober. In fact, I told myself, he might be a nice change of pace from all the Captain America, Big Man on Campus, Mr. Perfects Betsy probably dated.

But could I do that to her? Set her up with Goober? That didn't seem fair.

Then I remembered that love is blind. Or is that justice? Maybe I was getting Cupid and the blindfolded lady with the scales mixed up in my head.

I was desperate; I had to find someone for Goober so that I could study the effects and outcome of a guy and girl interacting in a date setting. And it was only a date, not an arranged marriage. I took comfort in the temporary aspect of that thought.

Now I had to figure out the best way to get a guy like Goober to appeal to a girl like Betsy. This was going to call upon all my powers of description and diplomacy. There was a time when I would have lied. But that had been a horrible disaster. So I'd go with the truth. I walked right over to Betsy's house before I chickened out.

She answered the door.

"Kev! Great to see you. What brings you by?"

"I need your help." I figured Betsy was the kind of person who would be touched by a blatant appeal.

"Oh, honey, sure. Anything for you and your family. What do you need?"

"I have a friend and I'd like you to go out with him. On a date."

"Hmmm." She studied me. "Normally, I'd say no, because I'm not a big fan of blind dates, but if my mother asks me to fill one more swan-shaped helium balloon or speak to the caterer one more time about the texture of the crab cakes, I'll lose my mind. She's going crazy with this party for my grandparents and making everyone around her nuts too. Can the date be this very minute?" She practically ran down the steps toward the sidewalk.

"Uh, sure, yeah," I panted, jogging to catch up, "if that works for you. I'll just, uh, call Goo—the guy and see if he can meet us at, um, the Juiceteria? Feel like a smoothie?"

"Always."

Yeah, me too. I wondered what I could put in Goober's smoothie to de-Goober him and make him seem like a great guy. But then again, Betsy was looking for any excuse to run away, so anyone might seem good in comparison to what she was running from. Timing really is everything in matters of scientific research. I'm sure Alexander Graham Bell, in retrospect, was glad he'd spilled acid on himself just before he called Watson. Made that first phone call in history more exciting than just "Can you hear me now?"

I texted Goober as Betsy and I walked to the Juiceteria, and he replied that he'd be "rite their." Oh, great. A spelling whiz.

Betsy and I were sitting at the table by the

window, sipping smoothies, when Goober rolled up. He'd gotten dressed for the date. He was wearing a white T-shirt with a picture of a tuxedo on it and, from the sound of things, he had on tap shoes.

"Are you wearing tap shoes?" I asked after I'd introduced them. Betsy, to her credit, hadn't flinched or pulled away.

"Yes. I thought I'd do a little routine for the lady."

"You thought tap dancing would make a good impression on a girl? Really?"

"Yeah, I'm great. Besides, I thought I should tap into my feminine side."

I pretended to laugh.

"I'd love to see you tap-dance," Betsy told him. I was sure she had a brain freeze from the smoothie, because what girl in her right mind wants some scruffy-looking guy dancing—loudly—for her in public?

Well, Betsy did. Even Betsy doesn't have good enough manners to fake the enthusiasm she demonstrated as she clapped for Goober.

He was pretty good. I was grinning and clapping along with Betsy. And the employees and customers of the Juiceteria.

"How do you do that?" I asked as his feet became a blur.

"I'll show you. Stand up. You too, Bets."

"Bets" leapt up and pulled me out of my chair. "Come on, Kev! Let's do it."

I agreed. Purely in the interest of scientific exploration, not because it looked like so much fun it would make a person squeak from joy.

"This," Goober said, demonstrating, "is a shuffle step. Now you." We tried. It was more shuffle than step, but it was awesome. A girl from behind the counter and two guys standing in line tried it as well.

"Okay, now go like this—toe-heel, heel-toe, and again. Right, good, follow me and stamp, ball change, again, drop, brush, swing, and shuffle-hop-step!"

"We're dancing. We're really dancing!" Betsy was grinning from ear to ear. I think I was too, but it was tough to know because I was concentrating so hard on keeping up with the steps Goober was demonstrating and wondering why my parents had never thought to get me tap-dancing lessons. Tap dancing rocked.

"How'd you get so good?" Betsy asked when we finally had to sit down to rest.

"Granny Barb taught tap and I learned when I was little."

"You're amazing."

"I know."

"When Kevin suggested we meet, I didn't have high hopes."

"Me either. Little buddy pulled a bait and switch on me earlier today—wouldn't set me up with his fine-looking mother."

"Mrs. Spencer is a lovely woman. I can see the attraction."

"You know it." They nodded at each other, bonding over my mother's good looks.

"You should come to Gran and Papi's anniversary party with me. They'd love it if you danced for them."

"Count me in." They smiled at each other while I tried to wrap my head around the fact that this crazy pairing seemed to work.

"Hey," Goober said to Betsy and definitely not to me, apparently invisible as I was behind my mango banana smoothie, "would you like to get a bite to eat? I'm hungry from all the dancing, and fro-yo and pulverized fruit isn't getting the job done."

Pulverized? Goober had used the word *pulverized*.

In a sentence. Correctly. And with good manners, charm and—even I had to admit—a winning smile? This was turning out to be a highly successful experiment, and coming as it did on top of the hockey team/figure skaters achievement of the prior evening, I was feeling my inner matchmaker blossom. Some people, I know, just have a flair for bringing together soul mates. And it's always fun to discover a new talent. I basked as Goober and Betsy deserted me at the Juiceteria.

8

The Scientific Mind Compares Science and Society

I was on a roll.

Both Daniel and Goober were happily coupled up. Well, I didn't know so much about happily, but now it was up to them to make the relationships work.

But they're guys, I thought. In keeping with my desire to set myself more difficult tasks and consequently learn greater lessons, it was time to try to find Mr. Right for some lucky girl.

Hmm . . . what girls did I know who would go along with my suggestion?

Connie Shaw. We'd had a small misunderstanding a while back when I used to lie, but we'd cleared the air. Plus, she's Tina's best friend and she's in my first-period class.

As luck would have it, we had a sub on Thursday morning. As long as we're quiet and there's no blood, most subs are happy just to keep us in the room until the bell rings. After attendance was taken, everyone broke into small study groups and I made a beeline for Connie.

"You're a great girl, did you know that?" I started. I didn't have time for subtlety.

"Uh, thank you. I think. What's going on?" Given my history, her skepticism was well placed. I didn't take it personally or let it dissuade me.

"I have the perfect guy for you to meet." Or I would as soon as she agreed and I discovered more about what she was looking for, guy-wise. Let me be clear: This was not a lie—it was a statement of optimistic planning. There's a difference.

"You do? The perfect guy? For me?"

"Absolutely. You in?"

"In for what?"

"A date."

"Oh, um, I'm kind of shy and I don't think I'd be—"

"I'll come with, to sort of smooth things over until you get your sea legs. It'll be great. Say yes."

Connie's something of a pushover.

"All right. When?"

"After school today?"

"Sure."

"Great. We'll go to the Juiceteria." Strike while the iron, and location, are hot. "I'll meet you at your locker after last period." That would give me just seven hours to find her a date. Too much time and I might overthink things, blow it. This kind of pressure was destined to bring out my best skills.

She nodded, doubtful. I got away from her fast so she couldn't change her mind.

I sat at my desk and started thinking. Very hard. Where was I going to come up with a guy for Connie? I considered and dismissed all my friends. They're great buddies but lacking in the sensitivity department. And Connie, while a nice person with a fine mind and a great personality, isn't, um, the prettiest girl I've ever met—if you're judging by conventional standards, that is. I'm sure there's a society somewhere that worships girls who look like

Connie. But my boys are dogs, they're not as refined and mature and broad-minded as I am.

It's a good thing I'm a curious person who files away random and seemingly inconsequential bits of information. You never know when you might need to use facts you've heard, and subconsciously absorbed, in passing.

Because, after a few moments of deep reflection, I remembered that Betsy's cousins were also coming to town for Gran and Papi's anniversary party. I sat quietly, breathed deeply and ran through the memory card in my head. Betsy's relatives. She had to have a cousin around my age. Well, she didn't have to, of course, but it would sure help if she did.

I slid my cell phone out of my backpack, hid it behind a textbook and surreptitiously texted Betsy: "dont u hav a guy cousin my age?"

Apparently she was clinging to her phone for life support, because the reply came immediately: "yes. didnt u meet him @ my grad party?"

I thumb-typed back: "no. is he cool like u+can I set him up on a date 2?"

She responded before I could move my thumb off the keyboard: "yes+yes. can I come w/?"

Me: "yes, Juiceteria @ 330."

Her: "we're leaving right now—kidding. but my mother is crazy, no joke."

Me: "more swans, rite? c u l8er."

My mind is like a steel trap. No, a NASA computer. No, words to describe my mind have yet to be invented.

The rest of the day dragged. I've noticed that time slows down between the origin of a good idea and the implementation of it. Downtime is no one's friend, and I wondered how all those scientists kept themselves from dying of boredom waiting for experiments to be completed.

And it didn't help that when I got to the cafeteria for lunch, Tina was sitting at my regular table. She never sits at my table. Probably avoiding Cash. I hoped. I didn't see him anywhere near her, and my spirits soared.

Luckily, I ducked behind a pillar before Tina spotted me in the doorway. I still hadn't learned enough to try one-on-one time with her yet. I didn't have sufficient data. I watched her for a few minutes and then headed to the library, where I ate my PB&J in a carrel and flipped open Mom's science book to convince myself I was doing all the right things to win Tina's heart. Yes! On the page I opened to randomly, my mother had underlined: "In periods of acknowledged crisis scientists have turned to philosophical analysis as a device for unlocking the riddles of their field."

I'm not sure exactly what the guy was talking about except that (a) I was in crisis, (b) girls were a riddle and (c) I was analyzing everything around me. Nothing like a fluorescent-yellow highlighter to point the way.

Finally the last bell rang and I grabbed Connie on the way out of school. She looked nervous and didn't say much on the walk to the Juiceteria.

I grinned from ear to ear when we walked in and spotted Betsy and her cousin. Connie frowned.

"He's wearing a Buket o' Puke 'n Snot T-shirt," she whispered.

"I know. He's perfect."

"I hate that band."

"How can anyone with ears hate that band? They're geniuses."

"They're disgusting."

"You're wrong. But"—I raised my hand to avoid the argument—"we're not here to discuss the world's most awesome band. We're here to introduce two great people to each other and see how it goes."

Betsy waved us over. The guy stood to greet us.

"Hey, good to meet you. I'm JC Tucker."

"I'm Kevin Spencer. This is Connie Shaw, my friend from school."

"You haven't met?" Connie sounded a little panicky.

"Not officially, but we're practically family," I said, stretching the definition of *family* a bit.

"Yeah, we're like brothers from other mothers," JC said, and he and I laughed. Connie frowned again. Betsy sighed. We all sat down.

"So, JC, you like Buket o' Puke 'n Snot?" I asked.

"Who doesn't?"

Connie, wisely, remained silent.

Betsy's phone rang. She looked at the screen and made a face as she read the message. "I have to go. A crisis about the ice sculpture in the shape of a swan." She stamped out of the Juiceteria. Connie looked stricken at having been deserted, and I grabbed her arm before she could flee. Apparently, she didn't think I was capable of facilitating her date with JC. I'd show her.

"Uh, Connie here is in student government," I told JC.

"Cool. I was too. Well, not really. I crashed a student government meeting once."

"So did I!"

"Crazy, huh? Hey, did you go to that huge Buket o' Puke 'n Snot concert a while back?"

"I had a ticket, but at the last minute I wasn't able to go."

"Me too! I got grounded."

"So did I. Wow, we have some stuff in common."

"Yeah," Connie said. "Are you thirsty? Should I go get us some smoothies?"

"Yeah, I'll have the banana mango—"

"With extra protein powder!" JC finished my order and we grinned at each other's great taste. Connie snorted and went up to the counter.

"Are you in town for long?" I asked JC.

"Just a few days. We came early so my mom could help Betsy's mom with the party. Betsy and I are going stir-crazy. We made over a hundred swans out of napkins this morning. The party's got a swan theme, I guess they mate for life or something. Creepy, right?"

"Birds make me nervous."

"That movie? The one where the birds fly in the chimney and attack the school and just generally go berserk, swooping around in mean, threatening flocks and trying to peck the eyes out of everyone?"

"Only the scariest movie ever."

Connie came back with our smoothies then, but JC and I barely noticed. JC and I talked about other scary movies that freaked us out and our favorite military battles and our fantasy football, baseball and basketball leagues. Connie started doing her homework.

"Do you play lacrosse?" JC asked.

"Only every weekend of my life."

"Could you use another middy this weekend?"

"Is the bird movie terrifying? Heck yeah. We're at Noble Park at ten on Saturdays, it's a pickup league and there's doughnuts. I'll swing by Betsy's house to get you."

He said, "Awesome, I'll see you Saturday. I better get back to the house, see if there are swan chocolate fountains or swan piñatas I should help with."

I watched him walk down the street and couldn't wait for the weekend.

"I kind of miss him already," I said to Connie as I walked her home.

"Uh-huh."

"That may well have been the greatest first date ever."

"For you."

"What are you talking about?"

"He didn't say a word to me."

"Oh. Well, uh, you weren't a Chatty Cathy yourself." I probably shouldn't have sounded so defensive.

"I couldn't get a word in edgewise."

I started to feel guilty. I'd forgotten all about Connie and how this was supposed to be her date.

We walked the rest of the way to her house in silence. The warm glow I'd gotten from meeting JC faded with each awkward step. When she went inside, Connie didn't say goodbye.

I didn't blame her.

9

The Scientific Mind
Never Misses the Obvious

I was sitting in homeroom the next morning, wondering how I'd let almost an entire week go by while accumulating only marginal knowledge about the best way to get Tina to notice me. Before Cash made her notice him. I'd been keeping an eye on Cash all week, and I didn't like how often he was near Tina. Plus, it was Friday—another two date nights were about to pass me by. Something had to change.

My process was taking too long. I needed to accelerate the momentum. I needed a larger control group, more data as fast as possible.

That was it! Of course.

Speed dating.

I'd read about that in the newspaper. A group of guys and women showed up at a bar or restaurant and shifted from table to table, meeting potential dates. They had a few minutes to get to know each other before a bell sounded and they moved on to the next person.

I'd have to figure out a way to round up a bunch of girls who don't go to my school. Because my buddies are great and all that, but there's no way I'd get the girls who know these guys to come out and speed-date with them. They pretty much won't give them the time of day in class.

I was running through a list of places where I could hold such an activity when the morning announcements started.

"Will someone—anyone—please volunteer to run the cakewalk at tonight's fun fair? The room is all set up, the baked goods have been delivered, we just need a warm body to start and stop the music and hand out the cakes to the winners."

My arm shot into the air and I leapt to my feet. *"I'll do it!"* I think my enthusiasm scared my homeroom class, not to mention my teacher.

"All right, Kevin, you may be excused to go to

the principal's office to offer your services. Head straight to first period afterwards."

Head straight to the Genius Hall of Fame is what she should have said to me. Because when the principal said "cakewalk" what I heard was "speed date." With a little finagling of the rules, plus girls from outside our school—our fun fair draws huge crowds from all over town every year—this was the perfect solution to my problem. In only eleven hours from now. More than enough time to work out the logistics and spread the word to my friends.

I told the school secretary that I was volunteering for cakewalk duty. "Great," she said, sounding like she thought it was anything but a good idea, as she handed me a laminated sheet. "Here are the instructions. Everything's set up in the art room. Be there at six-thirty to bring the baked goods over from the cafeteria's walk-in fridge. You'll need some assistance, because there are about forty plates of cakes, cupcakes, brownies and bars. The cakewalk runs from seven to nine and the fair closes at ten."

I was walking down the hall, reading the instructions and thinking: How do I change the rules so that kids will win one-on-one time with a member of the opposite sex rather than a Boston cream pie? I heard my name and I turned my head.

Tina. She was showing Cash where the gym is.

How long is it going to take him to find his way around, anyway? I thought. It's a middle school, not the Pentagon.

I was so rattled at the sound of Tina's voice and the sight of her and Cash together that I kept walking straight ahead and plowed into a stack of boxes. In my defense, the school hallway seldom has boxes of fun-fair prizes standing around. I don't know what was in those boxes, bricks maybe, because they didn't give and I caromed off the cardboard and lost my footing on the laminated instructions I'd dropped, and crashed to the floor.

All I ever do when Tina's around is wind up flat on my back.

"Wow." She pushed her incredible, silky, bouncy hair off her perfect face and put out a hand to help me up.

Before her skin could touch mine, that lunkhead Cash reached down and yanked me to my feet. "Dude. Gotta be more careful." Clearly, he was loving my embarrassment.

"That looked like it hurt," Tina said. "I'm really sorry I startled you like that. Are you okay?"

"Uh . . ."

"What a silly place to put boxes, huh? Who'd expect them in a crowded hallway during passing time?"

"Um . . ."

"Are you going to the fun fair tonight?" she asked.

"Oh, well, I don't know, I mean, I hadn't thought—I mean, probably, although I'm not sure. . . . I'll have to see what JonPaul and the guys say."

"Oh, so you're going with your friends?"

I think I nodded. I hope I didn't just keep staring at her.

"I was thinking about going too."

"Oh, good. I'm running the cakewalk."

"I thought you said you weren't sure if you were going?" Cash jumped in.

"Well, uh, did I? I mean, yes, I did. That's because, um, I wasn't sure if I was going to go, but now I am, and so I'll be there. At the fair. Walking the cake run. I mean running the walkcake. I mean, the cakewalk." I felt this horrible smothering feeling, like the air had turned gelatinous, and I gulped a few loud breaths, trying to get my lungs functioning again.

A long, awkward silence. Tina looked at me; Cash looked at himself in the glass of the fire extinguisher case; I felt myself sweat.

"Class!" I didn't think I'd shouted, but Tina and Cash jumped at my bellow. "We're late for class. We've got to get to first period."

I ran down the hall toward class, but I heard her call after me, "See you at the fair tonight, Kev."

The whole rest of the day I worked on the particulars of a speed date and how to attract a crowd while flying under the adult radar. Good thing I'm always up for a challenge. I did what marketers have done since the beginning of time: I counted on word of mouth and the appeal of the forbidden to draw a suitable audience.

"Kevin's setting up speed dates with the cutest people from other schools at the cakewalk tonight. Pass it on." By lunchtime, someone had even told *me* about the speed date/cakewalk that I couldn't miss. Everyone was psyched.

I studied the laminated cakewalk instruction sheet. Basic info—numbers had been taped to the floor. People walked from one number to another while the music played. When the music stopped, the master of ceremonies, me, drew a number from a bowl, and the person with the winning number got the cake. Easy enough and plenty of room for improvement to suit my purposes.

What I decided to do was to have two concentric circles, one pink for girls and the other blue for boys. When the music played, the boys' circle would move to the left, the girls' circle to the right; when the music stopped, everyone had one minute to meet and talk to the person opposite them. From time to time, I'd call numbers and give away cakes to keep from getting stuck with a mountain of devil's food.

It was a good day to be me. I'm sure everyone felt that way.

I got there early to bring the cakes to the room from the cafeteria refrigerator and set them on the display tables and tape down the colored circles. It didn't take much work to put my brilliant plan into motion.

I had a line of customers out the door and down the hall as soon as the fair started. I was turning the music on and off and pulling numbers as fast as I could. I looked up and saw that Katie had arrived and had taken over handing out bakery stuff to the winners for me. I waved a thank-you to her and she nearly dropped a cake before turning away quickly.

Sparks flew all over the place. I had to be the most popular event at the whole fun fair. I'd never seen so many people in one room before. And everyone was having a good time and meeting new people except my buddies, who were standing at the side of the art room like the wall all of a sudden needed a lot of help to stay upright.

What is wrong with these guys? I thought. They can't just stand there, they have to exert themselves, be a part of what's going on around them. If it's one thing I hate, it's people who miss the obvious.

Tina walked into the room just as things were getting really crazy. "Hey, Kev, great event." At least I think that's what she said; the room was so loud that I couldn't eavesdrop on my buddies Dash and Wheels, who were finally talking to the cute blondes from St. Agnes. How was I supposed to collect information about talking to girls?

At least I didn't fall over or say something stupid.

And I'd watched Cash collect phone numbers from a ton of girls who went to different schools. What a flirt. Tina will thank me someday for setting up the cakewalk and showing her his true colors. If, of course, she even remembers him once we're a couple.

10

The Scientific Mind
is Sometimes clueless

Upon reflection, the speed-dating thing on Friday night had been a horrible debacle—for me, at least. I'd been so busy that I hadn't learned anything of value, and the face-to-face thing, for me if not for everyone else, hadn't worked out. My buddies Dash and Wheels, though, had dates for Saturday night with the St. Agnes girls they'd met on numbers 25 and 16.

I hadn't slept all night and was up really early Saturday morning, pacing around my bedroom. I called in sick to work because I knew I needed a new brilliant idea. I'll be honest, I was starting to freak out.

I was wandering around my room, deep in thought, when I tripped over my computer cord.

I had it: Computer dating.

I was seeing the commercials on television all the time, so it had to work. Not that I wanted to meet anyone on the computer—I'd already met the girl of my dreams—but I could study a site and learn, because I needed help quick and what's quicker than the Internet? Nothing.

I logged on to a site and started reading the questionnaire: "Where do you want to be in 5 years?" Dumb question—I want to be a freshman in college, and I can barely figure out where I'll be five hours from now.

"Do you want children?" Uh no, ick. I'd made a mess of the flour baby project in social studies last term; I was supposed to pretend the sack of flour was a baby and never put it down, but I kept losing mine. I was clearly not father material, at least not at this time.

I scanned the rest of the questions, and all that did was make me more panicky than ever because I realized that if I didn't land Tina now and lock her down on the forever-after thing, my future would be filled with serious questions about political and religious beliefs, my feelings about money and material possessions, and my goals and aspirations. Snore. I had to get Tina to be my girlfriend before she started wanting to know about all that boring stuff.

The dating site was the dumbest thing I'd done yet, and I was discouraged for a second. But then I remembered that not all experiments prove their hypotheses, and that frequently the results gained, although not what was expected, are still valuable. That must have been what had happened here. And the book about science said it was important to know when to abandon a faulty line of thinking. I shut down the computer, grabbed some leftover pizza from the fridge and headed off to pick up JC at Betsy's house and play lacrosse. Nothing like whacking the crap out of your opposition with a stick to clear a guy's head.

I had a great morning. My team got creamed, but it didn't really matter because guys are so easy to get along with. You never have to worry about what they're thinking or how they're feeling. You just have to pass the ball and get out of the way.

JC was an awesome player—fast, didn't hog the ball or try to make points when he should have been giving an assist. We had a blast. It was the first truly peaceful time I'd spent all week. I was bruised and battered after the game—it's a rough sport and I felt like I'd been pummeled—but I was ready to go out there and try a new approach to winning Tina's heart.

Because I'd seen that some of the guys had girl-friends on the sidelines and I wanted Tina to stand on the edge of the field and watch me play lacrosse. It would be so great, and I had a feeling deep in my gut that it was my destiny. I couldn't give up now. No matter how discouraged I was, I had to press on. True scientists never, ever quit.

As I walked home from the lacrosse game, I faced a cold, hard truth: I still had no idea what-soever what girls thought about guys and dating. Maybe the secret of figuring out romance wasn't to study couples or guys alone or even to try to set up another girl on another date, but to get inside a girl's head. It was time for me, Kevin Lucas Spencer, to get out there and ask direct questions. Maybe. Go directly to the source and speak to a real girl I actually know. A girl who knows everything and has answers to all the questions and a few that haven't been asked yet.

I was going to ask Katie Knowles for help.

She's frighteningly brilliant. The only reason I hadn't gone to her again since lunch on Monday was that she doesn't like me. Well, truth be told, she hates my stinking guts. I'd have to be a fool not to notice the way she squinched up her eyes real tight and wrinkled her nose like I smelled bad and looked right through me when I was near her. Except that I'd noticed, this past week, that she was starting to warm up to me.

We have a history of . . . unfortunate misunderstandings, and she holds a grudge. Well, actually, she feels I take advantage of her every time I can, and she isn't wrong.

But this was different; I wasn't going to try to get her to do anything, and she'd be flattered that I was turning to her for answers. People like to think you think they're smart. And Katie really is. I've seen her stump teachers.

I texted her: "u free 4 a smoothie?"

She didn't respond in the spirit in which I made the offer: "WHO IS THIS?"

Geez, even her texts sound bossy. But she probably didn't have my number in her address book. However, that was about to change. I was going to learn about girls and put things right between Katie and me. I am a great multitasker.

I texted back: "Kev." I left off the "duh." "ill b rite over 2 get u."

Then I turned off my phone in case she was going to text back "NO NEVER."

She looked nervous when she answered the door. I figured it was because she didn't want her neighbors to see her with me. I almost offered to walk ten feet ahead of her so no one would think we were together. I'm a thoughtful guy.

We headed to the Juiceteria and I made a mental note: Next time ask for some sort of discount for bringing in all this business. Katie said thank you when I paid for her smoothie. Making peace is always a good idea.

"What did you want to talk to me about?" she asked. If I hadn't known better, I'd have sworn she was a little shy.

"I have feelings for someone and I don't know what to do." Best I just blurt out the truth so there would be no room for misunderstanding.

"You have feelings?"

"Yes."

"For a girl?"

"Yes."

"Why are you telling me?"

"Who else could I tell?"

"Oh . . ."

"I'm a little embarrassed because I don't know what to say or do and . . . this girl . . . is so obviously better than me that I don't even know where to start to tell her how amazing and smart and beautiful she is."

"Oh." Katie looked at me for a long moment, took a breath and then said, in a soft voice, "I think I understand your dilemma."

"You do?"

"Yes . . . and I feel the same way."

"You do?"

"I didn't know until earlier this week when you came over to sit with Connie and me during lunch, but once you put it out there and I examined my own feelings, well, I guess if you can come clean, so can I."

Whoa.

"What are you talking about?"

"You. Me." She blushed and dropped her eyes. Oh no. "Us."

She thinks we're on a date?

She's fallen for me?

How can this be possible?

Hunh.

I should have recognized that my charm could be overpowering. Also, I'd asked her out, picked her up at home and paid for her smoothie.

Okay. Be delicate, sensitive, pick the right words, let her down easy, show her how concerned and caring a guy I am.

"Oh, hey, hold on there, you've got this all wrong. I just meant to pick your brain because you're the smartest—"

"Pick. My. Brain." I'm sure there are surgical scalpels less pointed than Katie's words.

"Uh, well, not exactly, I know that sounds a little harsh—"

"Not as harsh as using me. A habit of yours."

"You've got me there." I smiled, trying for charming self-deprecation.

"I should have known you were setting me up again."

"No! Wait, I never meant—"

"You never mean anything, Kevin, that's the problem."

I opened my mouth, but she cut me off. "I

was an idiot to forget that you always have ulterior motives."

She got up so fast she bumped the table, knocking over both of our cups. She left and I sat there with a lapful of smoothies. Once again, I'd messed everything up. I don't know how this keeps happening to me, but as Katie said, it's become a habit.

Not my best one, either.

11

The Scientific Mind
could Learn a Lot from Markie

I know that Auntie Buzz believes that divorce is a very special thing between a man and a woman and it should not be trifled with by outsiders, but I couldn't help noticing that Markie's parents didn't seem so divorce-friendly all of a sudden.

They were sitting in the kitchen talking, instead of both clearing out of Markie's house while I was babysitting Saturday afternoon.

After the scene in the Juiceteria with Katie, I'd slunk home, taken a shower and changed. I was feeling really down and was happy when Markie's mom called, asking if I was free to babysit. I was looking forward to an afternoon with Markie. No matter what's going on, he always makes me feel better.

It really *is* Markie's house now; since his parents split up, they take turns moving in and out according to their custody schedule. They rented an apartment a few blocks away. When I got to the house that afternoon, Markie's dad had just pulled up and Markie's mom was about to leave—they both carried overnight bags—but they both looked like they had no place else better to go but weren't about to send me home either. I guessed I could keep Markie occupied while they talked.

Markie's parents.

Interesting.

That would be my next experiment: to reunite Markie's parents! Granted, I'd never broken up with anyone and I wasn't planning to ever break up with Tina once we got together, but this could be a good chance to collect some useful relationship information.

I wasn't going to make the same mistake I'd made with my parents and try to orchestrate quality time. Markie's parents looked happy enough just sitting at the table. But what if I helped to remind them of the good times? I could do that. I sat in their living room and tried to come up with a way to bring those old feelings back for them.

Markie was still talking about the Serengeti documentary. "... and then the dung beetle rolls up dung— the man on the movie said dung is feces, but it looked like poopies to me, Dutchdeefuddy. Some of them eat the dung, some bury it and some live in it. Ick."

Markie.

Parents go all soft and mushy over their babies. Markie was a little too old now, and a whole lot too loud, and way too gross, to make his parents all sentimental. But there had to be baby pictures somewhere in the house. I am awesome at presentations. I have never gotten anything less than an A– when poster board is involved. So—bazinga! I'd make a poster of the life and times of Markie's family. Guaranteed to melt his parents' hearts.

"Markie!" He was sitting on the floor, drawing pictures of bugs and turds.

"What, Dutchdeefuddy?"

"Baby pictures of you, bud. Where are they?"

"In the basement. C'mon, I'll show you. Can I help?"

"Counting on it, big guy, couldn't do it without

you." He beamed and took my hand, leading me downstairs to a small room with a large table and an even larger collection of shoe boxes. Full of pictures. I started going through the boxes, which were dated and arranged in chronological order. Markie's mother had apparently taken enough photographs of Markie that I could make a flip book of them and see him crawling across the living room floor, inch by inch. On the shelves behind the table were a couple dozen empty photo albums and about four cubic tons of colored paper, stickers, fancy scissors and something called "archival-quality" glue, all still in their packages. Clearly, Markie's mom had intended to scrapbook Markie's entire life. Why she didn't just leave them on the computer and make a slide show as her screensaver like any normal twenty-first-century citizen, I'll never know. But moms can be old-fashioned about "preserving memories." I only know that phrase because there was an open book next to the shoe boxes, *Preserving Memories for a Lifetime: Scrappin' with Salley Sue Sullivan.*

I'd pull a sampling of photos of happy times with Markie and his folks and make a poster, reminding them how a divorce would mess that up forever. I could use a flattened cardboard box as the poster board.

"Okay, let's find some vacation pictures and holidays and special events." Markie started pawing through the boxes next to me.

"Here." Markie handed me a picture of him as a mini-toddler screaming bloody murder on his father's lap; his face was all red and his mouth wide open midscream, and he was twisting out of his dad's grip, trying to get away.

"Oh, um, really? You want this picture?"

"Yeah, it's funny."

"Okay, but try to find some pictures of you guys on vacation at the beach or in front of the Christmas tree. You know, something fun."

"Here." He thrust out a photo of him as a baby, sleeping in his crib with his butt in the air in that weird way babies do, sucking his thumb.

"Kinda boring, isn't it?"

"I look happy." And, I thought, I'm sure your folks were happy you weren't making any noise. Wise choice.

I kept searching through the boxes, starting to get a little frantic that I couldn't find the quintessential pictures of good times.

"Here." Markie was smiling at a picture of his parents sitting on deck chairs in the backyard. At least I think it was his parents; it was kind of hard to tell because their heads had been cropped off. "I took this."

"Cool, headless zombie parents." Markie's eyes widened and I hurried to say: "Sorry, buddy, I didn't mean that. It's a great picture."

He started bouncing up and down in that way that means he's either really excited or I'm about to have to find him dry cargo pants. "Put some of my art with the pictures!"

"Couldn't hurt; go get your stuff, Picasso, and let's see what we can do."

What was with these people? I had never seen a more boring collection of photos, and that included my Great-aunt Blanche's daily pictures showing how her knee replacement scar healed. I was looking at a picture of Markie's parents' car when Markie trundled back downstairs with a cardboard box.

"Here's my turkey that I made tracing my hand for Thanksgiving. See, my preschool teacher wrote all I told her I was thankful for on the finger-feathers: Mommy and Daddy, Dutchdeefuddy, saying the alphabet in burps, TV and the loud noise I make when I bang on my wagon with a shovel."

"Now you're getting what I'm looking for, Markie. Good job, pal."

"I want this on the poster too."

"What is it?" I looked at a ripped and crumpled piece of paper with some crayon scribbles on it. "It doesn't look special."

"Not everything special looks special," he told me.

"What?" As usual, Markie was on to something.

"Sometimes the best things aren't perfect. That's what Miss Rita says at preschool. She says: 'Don't worry about doing things right, just have fun.'"

Markie's like a little Dalai Lama to me sometimes, he really is.

Just then we heard his parents laughing upstairs. Markie and I smiled at each other. I glanced down, surprised to see that we'd somehow covered the cardboard poster with pictures and artwork. It didn't look amazing, but it looked real.

Maybe I'd leave well enough alone for now. I glued everything down and propped the poster in the corner of the craft room; Markie's mom would find it eventually, though from the sound of them laughing, maybe Markie's folks didn't need my help.

"Let's go to the park," Markie said.

"Exercise and activity. Good idea."

We walked to the park three blocks over. I know how important it is for kids to get fresh air. Plus that archival-quality glue was giving me a headache.

Markie ran to the sandbox. I sat on the park bench and thought about all that I'd learned, or not, about guys and girls in the past week. I was deep in thought about why it seemed so complicated to me when everyone else was falling in love as easily as I fall over, when I looked up to see Markie hit a little girl between the shoulder blades with an empty bucket. I jumped off the bench and hustled over.

"Markie! Say you're sorry."

"But I'm not."

"You're not sorry you hit her with a bucket?"

"No."

"Why not?"

"I wanted her to play with me."

"That's not the way to do it."

"But look!"

The little girl handed Markie his bucket and they started building a castle together. Or maybe a dinosaur. Hard to determine the artistic intent of preschoolers.

"This is Maisie," he said, pointing a shovel at her.

"The line-butter from preschool who pinches you?"

He nodded.

"And you just hit her with a bucket?"

He handed Maisie the shovel.

"But now you're playing together."

"Sure." I could tell from his voice that Markie was starting to think I was really slow on the uptake.

They looked content, and they were together. Which was more than I could say about me and Tina.

The kid had a plan, he worked the plan, he reaped the results. Markie has always had a way of cutting to the heart of the matter for me. I think he might be my spiritual leader. I was going to have to buy him an ice cream cone. It was the least I could do.

12

The Scientific Mind Strives to Make Concluding Observations

The Putnams are very popular people, and I guess fiftieth wedding anniversaries are big deals. On Sunday morning, everyone I'd ever met in my entire life seemed to be eating brunch at Gran and Papi Putnam's anniversary party.

It was nice to see everybody, and Gran and Papi were having a blast, but to me the party was like Noah's ark. Everyone was paired up, two by two. I sat at a corner table in the catering hall, surrounded by swan decorations, eating bacon-wrapped scallops on little toothpicks and observing the romantic behavior around me.

Sir Isaac Newton's Third Law of Motion states

that for every action, there is an equal and opposite reaction. Although I had gotten no closer to Tina, my research and observation had apparently caused people around me to fall in love, or *more* in love.

My mother and father sat next to each other at a table near the swan cake with Markie's parents. My mother removed the strawberries from my father's plate with an exasperated look and handed him a couple of allergy pills, just in case.

"You split up?" My dad sounded surprised. He's never up on the neighborhood gossip. "I didn't know that. But I'm glad to hear you're trying to put your problems behind you."

They were joined by Auntie Buzz and her date, Jack, from the bank where she'd gotten a business loan.

Auntie Buzz came over and whispered to me: "What can I say? You got me thinking about my personal life, and I decided it was time to put myself back on the market. All this awesomeness shouldn't be unavailable." Although he wasn't anywhere near as hyper as Buzz, Jack seemed like a nice guy, and I noticed that he'd snagged a coffeepot from one of the waiters for the two of them to share. I tried to picture him as Uncle Number Four.

Sarah and Doug were helping to pass out hors d'oeuvres. Or rather, Doug was carrying the trays and Sarah was directing him. "Three o'clock, Doug. Sweep around to the three o'clock position with the cheese puffs." Doug headed toward nine o'clock, but everyone always needs more finger food, so Sarah didn't jump on his back. Some people are natural-born leaders, and others were meant to follow. Good thing they'd found each other.

Daniel and his hockey pals had taken over a table with the Welsh girls and the Connor sisters and were comparing ice schedules.

JonPaul and Sam were laughing and eating crêpes with our buddies Dash and Wheels and the girls from St. Agnes.

Katie and Connie (who'd been avoiding eye contact with me) and JC were learning to tap-dance from Goober and Betsy. Pretty soon, all five were tapping up a storm in the corner for Gran and Papi, who looked wildly impressed.

You're welcome, everybody, I thought, and the tap dance makes up for the fact that I forgot to sign the card with the present my mother bought Gran and Papi. My gifts might be spontaneous and even unintended, but they are quite meaningful.

Even Markie and Maisie LeBeau were hiding under a banquet table with all the swan balloons they'd collected from around the room. I kept an eye on Markie, but he didn't seem in danger of slugging her again. Besides, he didn't have a bucket.

I tried to be happy for them all, I tried not to be bitter. But it did sting a little that even Markie, who can't control his bladder a hundred percent of the time, and Buzz, who can't control what she says a hundred percent of the time, had found someone special.

I was the only person in the room, maybe in this town, perhaps in the Western Hemisphere, not living happily ever after. Well, Connie and Katie and JC had struck out too, but self-pity isn't nearly as effective when you have to think of other people, so I tried to ignore them.

I'd read about scientists being steadfast and self-confident and determined and unwavering. I'd never read about any of them feeling sorry for themselves.

I needed to do what I always do when I don't know what else to do: I needed to talk to my parents.

13

The Scientific Mind
Is No Match for Action

I found them at the chocolate fountain. My dad was eyeing the strawberries, but my mother skewered a piece of angel food cake on a stick and handed it to him. She stabbed a marshmallow, and I made a kabob of banana slices. We stood dipping for a little while. Some families bond over board games or trips, but melted chocolate brings the Spencer family together. We loaded our plates with chocolate-covered stuff on sticks and headed to an empty table.

"So, what's on your mind, son?" My dad always surprises me; you get to thinking he's not the sharpest tack on the board and then he goes all aware and thoughtful on you.

"Love."

"What about it?"

"I don't get it."

"No one really does. It's a mystery."

"All evidence to the contrary, you mean?" He raised an eyebrow and I explained. "Everyone at this party has a date. Except me."

"Did you ask someone?"

"Well, no. I was too busy."

"Too busy doing what?"

"Creating experiments so that I could learn about love and romance and being part of a couple and what girls want and how guys should act."

"Why?"

"I was examining behavior to gather the subjective and intuitive components of knowledge."

"How'd that turn out?"

"The preliminary results have been, thus far, abysmal."

"Sounds to me like you were trying too hard."

"I doubt that's possible. I was trying to apply the rules of science to figuring out what makes girls tick."

"I'd suggest personal inspection at zero altitude."

"What does that mean?"

"It means that to know about a girl, you have to spend time with that girl. You have to pay attention to what's in front of you; you can't turn matters of the heart into clinical observations."

"Scientific, Dad, not clinical."

"Feelings can't be studied and dissected like a frog, Kevin. You have to open yourself up to what's going on."

"That sounds awful."

"What's awful is if you're not present in the moment. You can't observe, you have to engage."

"You mean I need to stop thinking so hard about how to talk to Tina and just start talking to Tina?"

"Your father is a wise man." Having swiveled her head back and forth, following our conversation, for several minutes, Mom finally spoke up. "And very romantic. You should listen to him. He knows what he's talking about. He married me, didn't he?"

I remembered everything people had been trying to tell me all week. Buzz and Sarah and Jon-Paul and even Markie—if you boiled down what they had been talking about, they'd been telling me to take it easy. I'd listened, but I hadn't heard what they'd been saying. Oh, snap! So that was what Mom meant when she said that to Dad. I totally got it now.

My friends and family are extremely wise people, now that I stop to think about it. They should be, though; they hang around me—it was bound to rub off on them.

I felt better than I had in a long time.

14

The Scientific Mind Is Self-correcting

The science book I'd read quoted Francis Bacon: "Truth emerges more readily from error than from confusion." I had stacked up a whole lot of errors and even more confusion and was more than ready for some truth. I couldn't wait to see what happened the next day at school. I was going to put myself in a Tina place as soon as I possibly could. I smiled at the thought of seeing her the next day and went up to the buffet line. Epiphanies always stimulate the appetite.

Before I got there, though, I saw Katie and Connie. If I was going to get up the nerve to talk to

Tina, then I had to face them, too. Talking to girls seemed the only way out of the mess.

I went over to their table. They both tried to pretend I wasn't there. They had every right to think I was bad news and ignore my very existence.

"I'm really sorry, Con, about the date with JC. I messed up and I hurt someone I like without meaning to."

She looked surprised. Then pleased. "Oh . . . thanks. That's a nice thing to say."

"Don't worry; next time I'll find you someone better."

"That's okay, Kev; I'm glad it worked out for you and JC, and I guess I figured out I'm not really ready to date yet."

"You're a great friend, you know that?"

"You too."

I already knew that, but it's always a good thing to hear.

One down. One to go.

"Katie." I turned to face her, even though she was still looking away from me. "I handled our conversation all wrong, just like I did the social studies project and the tutoring service. Friends don't keep using friends to get what they want."

"We're not friends."

"Yeah, we are. At least I think so."

I could tell she was thinking hard, but she didn't know what to say.

"You didn't deserve how I treated you. I wanted to ask for your advice because I value your input. But I can see now where you may have read things differently than I intended. It's my fault, and I'm sorry if I embarrassed you."

"You've changed. A little," Katie told me.

"You have no idea," I said.

"You really think of us as friends?"

"Yeah, I do. And even though you don't feel that way right now, I hope you'll come around to it someday."

"Don't hold your breath." But she smiled, a little, as she said it.

I finally made a girl smile. Not the right one and not for the reasons I had in mind, but it felt good. *I* felt good. Finally, progress on the girl front. Maybe things were beginning to fall into place for me.

I knew enough to leave before I said something stupid and ruined the good thing I'd just done. I was in line with a plate in my hand when I heard:

"Kevin."

I looked up and saw Tina.

Tina. Here. Standing next to me. Right this very minute. I'm sure it was a trick of my eyes, but it looked like she was standing under a spotlight and, I don't know, glittering somehow. I sighed. I'd never been so happy to stand next to someone in my entire life.

"I've been trying to get your attention at school for a few days now," she told me.

"You have?"

"I'd been hoping we could come to this party together, since our families know the Putnams. I knew we'd both be here, and I thought it would be fun to come together."

"Really?"

"Uh-huh."

"Like a date?"

"Yeah. You seemed so distracted, though. Is everything all right?" She smiled at me and that tight, weird knot that usually forms in my gut when I'm near her and about to say something stupid or fall over melted away. I smiled back at her.

"Everything is perfect," I said.

Gary Paulsen is the distinguished author of many critically acclaimed books for young people, including three Newbery Honor Books: *The Winter Room, Hatchet,* and *Dogsong.* He won the Margaret A. Edwards Award given by the ALA for his lifetime achievement in young adult literature. Among his Random House books are *Paintings from the Cave; Flat Broke; Liar, Liar; Masters of Disaster; Woods Runner; Lawn Boy; Lawn Boy Returns; Notes from the Dog; Mudshark; The Legend of Bass Reeves; The Amazing Life of Birds; The Time Hackers; Molly McGinty Has a Really Good Day; The Quilt* (a companion to *Alida's Song* and *The Cookcamp*); *How Angel Peterson Got His Name; Guts: The True Stories Behind* Hatchet *and the Brian Books; The Beet Fields; Soldier's Heart; Brian's Return, Brian's Winter,* and *Brian's Hunt* (companions to *Hatchet*); *Father Water, Mother Woods;* and five books about Francis Tucket's adventures in the Old West. Gary Paulsen has also published fiction and nonfiction for adults. His wife, Ruth Wright Paulsen, is an artist who has illustrated several of his books. He divides his time between his home in Alaska, his ranch in New Mexico, and his sailboat on the Pacific Ocean. You can visit him on the Web at GaryPaulsen.com.

Gary Paulsen is available for select readings and lectures. To inquire about a possible appearance, please contact the Random House Speakers Bureau at rhspeakers@randomhouse.com.

Other terrific stories about Kevin

Available in hardcover from
Wendy Lamb Books
ISBN 978-0-385-74001-2

Available in paperback
from Yearling
ISBN 978-0-375-86611-1

Available in hardcover from
Wendy Lamb Books
ISBN 978-0-385-74002-9

Available in paperback
from Yearling
ISBN 978-0-375-86612-8

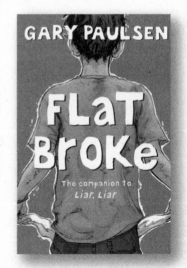